the
HOUSESITTER

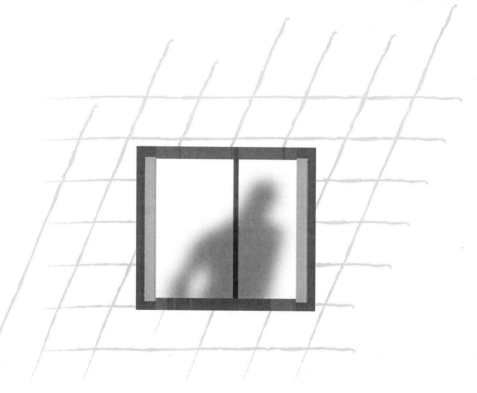

by
Cynthia Baxter

THE HOUSESITTER

Published by Dark Corridors
An imprint of SLM Bookworks
11 Peel Street
Selkirk, NY 12058

ISBN-13: 978-1614620037
ISBN-10: 1614620032

HOUSESITTER WANTED

Neat, responsible, non-smoker

Must like cats

Great location (Pasadena)

Beautiful house w/ big kitchen, WIFI, swimming pool

Need as soon as possible

Call John

626-555-1487

CHAPTER 1

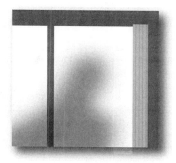

She rushed into Peet's, checking her watch as she breezed through the back entrance. She hurried past the dark wooden shelves stacked with ceramic mugs and coffee beans tightly packed in shiny, colorful bags. Glancing around, she saw that only a few people were sitting inside. Most customers had opted for one of the small round tables out front. Not surprising, since it was such a beautiful day—not to be taken for granted in October, a month that could be unpredictable, weather-wise, in southern California.

No one else was waiting to order, so she made a beeline for the counter. She ordered a regular coffee, quicker than her usual latte or cappuccino, then scanned the outdoor tables through the window.

Only one had a single occupant. A man at a table for two, looking around expectantly.

Peering through the glass, she let her eyes meet his. His eyebrows immediately shot up, asking a question. She nodded in response, then smiled. Clasping her coffee, she headed back outside, to his table.

"You must be John," she said.

"I am," he replied. "And you must be Megan."

"Pleased to meet you." She put her cup down and reached across the table to shake his hand.

As he half-rose to his feet, she studied him. He looked as if he was a few years older than she was, probably around forty. Tall, at least six feet. Fit, too, as if he belonged to a gym but didn't make working out his religion. He was dressed casually in khaki pants and a crisp, pale blue button-down shirt. His dark blond hair bordered on shaggy, and his smile was tentative, almost shy.

The most remarkable thing about him—the only remarkable thing—was his eyes. They were light colored, a pale hazel. But it wasn't their unusual shade that struck her. It was the intense way they bored into hers, as if he was looking deep inside her.

Evaluating her.

Of course he is, she thought. The man is trying to decide whether this total stranger who answered his ad for a housesitter is someone he can trust with all his earthly possessions.

"You're right on time," John observed. "That's a good sign."

"I'm one of those ridiculously reliable types," Megan replied as she sat down opposite him, dropping her oversized pocketbook next to her. "It drives some people crazy. When somebody tells me to meet them at eleven, I find the idea of showing up even one minute after completely unacceptable."

"Excellent," he said. "That you're such a responsible person, I mean."

She spilled a packet of sugar into her coffee, then stirred it. "I'm actually a little nervous," she confessed. "About meeting you, I mean."

"Why? It's not like this is a job interview. Or a date."

She flipped back her shoulder-length brown hair, then felt her cheeks grow warm as she realized she was acting *exactly* as if she was on a date. A blind date. Set up by someone who knew them both. Someone who thought they'd make a great pair.

But that wasn't what this was about. Not at all.

No romance here. Just a place to live for a while without having to pay any rent. Someplace different, somewhere that was completely outside her usual sphere. A place where she could get her head together. Where she could get her *life* together.

"Still, I have to ask you a few questions," he said, sounding apologetic.

"Of course." She kept her eyes fixed on his as she sipped her coffee.

"Where are you living now? You mentioned on the phone that you'd recently moved out of your old place."

"I'm not really living anywhere." Realizing how bad that sounded, Megan explained, "I've only been in L.A. for a few months. Last spring I moved here to take a job with Hayworth Insurance. I'd been working for them on the East Coast, but I came here to their corporate headquarters to work in their marketing department.

"I was subletting a place in West Hollywood," she continued, "but the lease ran out at the end of last month. It was right around the time I got laid off, along with about thirty other people." She laughed nervously. "It seems I've suddenly found myself at a sort of crossroads in my life."

Realizing that she'd just admitted to having no job and no place to live, she quickly added, "But I'm trying to look at this period as something positive. As a challenge. I've cut my ties to the past, and I'm free to redesign my life however I choose. It's actually kind of exciting, when you think about it."

John's expression remained noncommittal. "So where have you been staying?"

She grimaced. "On my friend Elissa's couch."

"Where's that?"

"Near Caltech, where she works."

"Ah," he said, his voice softening. "So you're already living here in the idyllic City of Roses."

Megan nodded. "Elissa's been really generous, but I'm starting to feel as if I've overstayed my welcome. She's been dropping hints about wanting her boyfriend to move in. Besides, it's not exactly the most comfortable situation in the world. I'm living out of a suitcase, with most of my stuff in boxes.

"So when I was at Speedy's yesterday and saw your ad on the bulletin board, I stopped in my tracks," she continued. "Given my situation—not knowing what I'll be doing next or where I'll be doing it—housesitting sounds like the perfect solution." With a sly smile, she added, "Especially at a house with a pool."

"Ah, yes, the pool." John paused just long enough to take a sip of his coffee. "There's nothing as relaxing as floating around on a raft, is there?"

"Actually, I'm a serious swimmer," she said. "At least I used to be. I was on my college swim team. I was pretty good, too." She let out a deep sigh. "Unfortunately, I've gotten away from it."

"It sounds as if you miss it," he observed.

"I do. Swimming has been a big part of my life. It's actually kind of strange, considering that I had a pretty traumatic experience in the water when I was a kid."

"What happened?"

"When I was seven, my family was at the Jersey shore with a bunch of relatives when there was a horrible accident. My nine-year-old cousin drowned."

Her voice thickening, Megan added, "I was pretty messed up about it. And absolutely terrified of getting back in the water again. But my grandparents had a beach house in North Carolina, and my parents were determined that I overcome my fears. They kept taking me back to the shore. Before long they couldn't get me out of the water. It turned out that when it came to swimming, I was a natural. I made it onto my high school swim team, then kept up with it in college . . . Anyway, as soon as I saw that your house had a pool, I was sold."

She stopped, suddenly self-conscious.

There I go, she thought, her cheeks burning. As usual, baring my soul to any Tom, Dick, or Harry I meet. As if this guy who's simply looking for a housesitter would be the least bit interested in every single detail about my life.

She was relieved that John didn't seem put off by her confession.

"The pool is amazing," he said. "One of the first things I did when I moved in was install a solar heating system, so you can pretty much use it year-round. In fact, the entire house is quite nice, if I do say so myself. It's got a huge kitchen and an unbelievable bathroom off the master bedroom. The people I bought it from redid practically the whole place just before they sold it."

"How long would you need me for?" she asked. Careful not to sound too eager, she added, "Or whoever you decide to go with?"

"I'm not sure, exactly. A few weeks, at least. Maybe longer." He frowned. "Would that be a problem? The uncertainty, I mean?"

"No," she answered quickly. "Not at all."

The two of them drank their coffee, allowing silence to fall over the table for a few seconds.

"Where are you going?" she asked, setting her cup back down. "Extended vacation?"

"No, I'm afraid it's just a work thing." He paused, taking another sip of his coffee. "My company is shipping me off to Minneapolis, of all places, for a special project."

"Wow. It gets really cold there."

"So I hear. But I have no choice. I've got to go wherever they send me."

"Aha," she said teasingly. "So you're one of those corporate types."

"Hardly." He pretended to shudder. "In fact, I've managed to arrange things so I mainly work from home."

"Who do you work for?"

"Kerwood Industries."

"Never heard of it." With a nervous laugh, she added, "Of course, I'm not exactly somebody who enjoys reading the *Wall Street Journal* every morning."

"What do you enjoy doing?" He leaned forward, fixing his eyes on her again.

Megan could feel her cheeks growing warm. Once again, she felt as if the two of them were on a blind date. The way they were slowly getting to know each other, feeling their way around, asking the questions they hoped would give them a sense of who the other was.

"I like writing," she admitted. It wasn't something she would tell just anybody. Then again, it wasn't as if John Davis was someone who'd be playing an important part in her life. He was just a man with a house she wanted to borrow for a while.

And a pool.

"In fact, I majored in English in college," she went on. "But writing isn't exactly the most practical thing in the world. I mean, a lot of people think they can write, especially in L.A. Even the guy who services my car is working on a screenplay."

"That doesn't surprise me," John said, smiling. Another swallow of coffee, then, "You know, while I was driving over here, I thought up all these great questions to ask you. But now that you're here, I can't remember any of them."

"I feel like I've already told you my entire life story." With a self-conscious laugh, Megan added, "Even what an upstanding, responsible person I am."

"Actually, there is one more thing I wanted to ask you," he said. "Is there anybody else who'd be staying in my house? Like a boyfriend?"

"No," she replied quickly. "There was, but not anymore."

"Ah. A sore point?"

"So it shows." She smiled sadly. "One more thing that ended a few weeks ago. That was when I finally realized it wasn't going anywhere. Or to be more accurate, that he wasn't going anywhere."

"Sorry."

"No, getting out of it was for the best." Her voice was strained as she added, "I'm not saying it was easy, just that it was something I had to do."

"Relationships can be tough," John commented.

"What about you?" she asked. "Are you married? Divorced? All of the above?"

He hesitated. "None of the above."

Megan just nodded, sensing reluctance to discuss his personal life.

"So I assume you like cats," John said.

Megan blinked. "Excuse me?"

"My cat? The main reason I need a housesitter?"

She realized she'd been so caught up in his ad when she'd spotted it at the copy shop that she hadn't bothered with the details. She'd simply pulled off one of the slips of fringe at the bottom, printed with his name and phone number.

"I love cats," she said. She placed her folded arms on the table and leaned closer. "Tell me about yours."

"Endora's great," he said. "I've had her for—let's see, going on five years now. I got her right after I moved in. She's gorgeous, with beautiful fur and a wonderfully intelligent expression." He smiled proudly. "Don't get me started on how terrific she is."

"What about her name?" Megan asked. "By any chance is she named after Samantha's mother in *Bewitched*?"

"Busted," he said, looking pleased that she'd picked up on the allusion. "Don't tell me you're also a fan of classic TV shows."

"Actually, I saw the movie a few years ago," she admitted. "The one with Nicole Kidman. I just happened to remember the name."

"You have a good memory," he said. "I guess I picked the name because Endora—I mean, *my* Endora—sometimes seems like she has special powers. More than most other cats, I mean. Like she's a good listener. When I pour my heart out to her, she seems to understand everything I'm saying."

John laughed. "At least, that's what I tell myself. But maybe I've just been living alone too long."

"Pets can easily become someone's family," Megan commented, anxious to show that she understood.

"Speaking of which, do you have family in the area?"

She shook her head. "They're all back east. Outside of Philadelphia, where I'm originally from."

"The Main Line?" he asked, naming one of the most exclusive residential areas on the East Coast.

"Not quite." She laughed, then stopped herself from flipping her hair over her shoulder again. "That's the *right* side of the tracks. I'm pretty much from the *other* side."

"Philly, huh? It must have been quite a change for you, moving out here to the West Coast all by yourself."

Picking up the wooden stirrer and running it around the edge of her cup, she said, "I have no regrets, even though I'm pretty much on my own out here."

"Still, it must be hard at times," he commented, "having no family around. Who do you spend holidays with?"

"I've made a few really terrific friends out here," she replied.

"It's not exactly like the old days, is it? Back when people lived in the same town their entire lives."

They both sipped their coffee, silent once again.

She finally asked, "So when do you expect to decide on a housesitter?"

"I think I already have," he said with a smile. "That is, if you're willing."

"That's great!" she exclaimed. "Now I guess I need to think up a bunch of things I should ask *you*."

"Why don't you stop by tomorrow—say, late morning?" John suggested. "You can ask me whatever questions you come up with between now and then. I can also show you around and tell you everything you need to know. The address is 55 Sierra Avenue, near the Huntington Gardens. Do you know that area?"

"I do. And I can use the GPS on my phone."

"Around eleven?"

"Perfect," she said with a satisfied nod. "Just out of curiosity, did anyone else apply? To housesit for you, I mean?"

"Yes, as a matter of fact," he replied. "Even though this whole thing has been so rushed, I've had a chance to interview a couple of other people."

"They didn't work out?"

He shook his head. "Trusting your house to a stranger—not to mention trusting your cat—is a big move," he said earnestly. "With something this important, you want to make sure you've found the right person."

CHAPTER 2

Megan was still marveling over her good fortune as she drove to John's house the next day. She'd opened all the car windows so she could relish both the warm sunshine and the cool morning air.

Pasadena had turned out to be a pleasant surprise. Since moving to L.A., she had noticed that for some reason, the upscale suburb was frequently the subject of ridicule among Angelinos—ironic, since the city of Los Angeles was basically a conglomerate of suburbs.

The old song "Little Old Lady from Pasadena" hadn't helped, reinforcing its reputation as a haven for rich, stuffy people. It also tended to get hotter than L.A. proper, and its geography had always made the air pollution worse than it was in the city.

Yet she'd felt at home here as soon as she'd moved into Elissa's. She appreciated the wide streets, the luxurious mansions, and the abundance of flowers and palm trees that gave the entire city the feeling of a resort community.

Pasadena's manicured beauty had gone a long way in restoring Megan's sense of balance. It had been a hellish few months. Just as she'd started coming to grips with being both unemployed and homeless, she was hit with the realization that something else in her life had to go: her relationship with Greg. In a very short time, everything in her life had been turned upside down.

Which was why she hoped that living in a house that was completely hers, at least for a while, would give her a chance to breathe.

Megan's heart fluttered excitedly as she turned onto Sierra Avenue. She drove along the wide residential street, noting the generous size of the lots as she studied each one, searching for house numbers.

John Davis's house turned out to be the last one on the block, located in the center of a small cul-de-sac. The house to the left was all but hidden behind a high hedge, an endless barricade of green. The one on the right had a vast, meticulously manicured lawn in front, the colorful profusion of flowers that lined the front punctuated by a big white For Sale sign.

Number 55 was a low white-stucco building with a red tile roof. It wasn't as big as some of the others on the street, but it was certainly a respectable size. At least as impressive as the house itself was the abundance of greenery that surrounded it: vibrant red and yellow flowers, dense bushes, and graceful palm trees that gave it the look of a jungle hideaway.

It's gorgeous, she thought with delight. She was even pleased by how isolated it was, deciding that could be exactly what she needed.

She pulled into the empty driveway and followed a narrow, winding walkway up to the front door, painted a bright orange-red that complemented the tile roof.

Then froze. She suddenly had the unnerving feeling she was being watched.

She whirled around. No one was there.

At least no one she could see.

Relax. Megan scolded herself. *You're just nervous because you've never done anything like this before. And you have to admit that the whole notion of housesitting is kind of strange. Moving into someone else's house—someone you don't even know—taking care of everything they own while they're out of town, acting as if you live there when you really don't . . .*

Still, she reminded herself, people housesat all the time. It was a win-win situation. The homeowners got someone responsible to look after their house while they were away and the housesitter got a free place to live.

Her confidence restored, she rang the bell. Melodious chimes echoed through the rooms inside.

John was smiling as he opened the door. He was wearing khaki pants, just like the day before, only this time with a navy blue polo shirt.

"You're right on time," he greeted her, running his hand through his dark blond hair as if he wasn't sure if he'd remembered to comb it that morning.

"I told you I'm ridiculously responsible," she said.

"Exactly the kind of person I want taking care of my house," he replied. "Come on in and I'll give you the fifty-cent tour."

She followed him inside, her heartbeat quickening as she saw just how sweet a deal she'd made.

The living room was large, with off-white carpeting, a long forest-green couch, and a sleek wooden wall unit that covered the entire wall opposite the front window. While it was dominated by a big screen TV, most of the shelves were crammed with books, CDs and DVDs, all neatly lined up. Displayed on some of the other shelves were decorative items like a white ceramic pitcher with hand-painted flowers and a tall glass vase.

"Wow," she said. "This is some place. It's much nicer than I expected. Not only the house, but also the landscaping. I really love flowers."

"Glad you like it." Turning, he announced, "And here comes the boss."

An unusually large, long-haired cat with orange fur, a bushy tail, and the bearing of a queen had wandered into the living room. She looked Megan up and down, as if considering whether to welcome her or give her the cold shoulder.

"Hey, Endora," Megan cooed, crouching down. "Aren't you a pretty kitty!"

Flattery appeared to work. The cat trotted over, meowing loudly.

"She likes you," John said, chuckling. "And believe me, that's not true of everybody. Hardly anybody, in fact."

"She's really gorgeous," she said sincerely as she stroked Endora's silky fur. "She must be some special breed."

"She is," John replied, sounding proud. "A Maine coon. Maybe I'm prejudiced, but I think they're the smartest of all cats. They make great companions, too. More like dogs than your usual stand-offish cats."

"I adore her already," Megan gushed. "I have a feeling we're going to get along just fine."

"Excellent. And now that you and the lady of the house have bonded, I'll show you around." Holding both arms out, John said, "This, if you haven't figured it out, is the living room. It's a pretty comfortable place to hang out, if I do say so myself."

"Very nice," Megan said, nodding. As if she were a potential buyer, taking a tour with a real estate agent, she politely added, "It's huge. And I can see that it gets lots of sun."

"This, obviously, is the dining room," John continued as Megan followed him into an adjacent area. It was also carpeted in off-white, furnished with a large table and six matching chairs. "Not that interesting—unlike the kitchen."

She knew what he meant as soon as they stepped into one of the largest kitchens she'd ever seen, with sage green walls, granite counters, and light-colored wooden cabinets. Even though it had a tremendous amount of counter space, in the center was a granite island. It was the same height as the counters, with two wooden stools on each side. Through the back door, she could see that the backyard was as lushly landscaped as the front.

"This is amazing!" she exclaimed. "I feel like I'm watching the Home and Garden channel!"

"Pretty nice, isn't it?" John agreed. "Unfortunately, I can't take any credit for it. As I mentioned, the previous owners renovated it right before they put it on the market. I was the beneficiary of their good taste—and their ample design budget."

"I'm not much of a cook," Megan admitted. "But maybe that's about to change."

"Be my guest," he said, waving his arm through the air as if offering her free rein of the place. "The house also has a couple of quirks I should tell you about. For some reason, the oven door sticks sometimes, and the temperature seems to be about twenty degrees cooler than whatever you set it at."

Gesturing toward the back door, he added, "One more thing: the lock on this door is kind of funky. I should probably get it replaced, but in the meantime, you've got to be sure it clicks into place when you close it or it won't stay shut." He grimaced. "Kind of a pain to remember all these nitpicky little things, but I can tell you're a quick study."

"I think I've got it," she assured him. "Oven door likes to stay shut, back door likes to stay open."

"Exactly," John said, nodding.

He showed her the cabinet where he stored Endora's food and gave her a quick lesson on how to feed her.

"And that about covers this room," he said. "On to the rest of the house."

As they walked down a long corridor, he pointed out a guestroom, a linen closet, a bathroom, and finally, the master bedroom. The two of them stepped inside, hovering by the door awkwardly.

"I wasn't sure whether you should stay in here or in the guestroom," John said, his eyes not meeting hers. "But then I figured you might as well make yourself comfortable. Not only is it the biggest and nicest bedroom in the house, it has its own bathroom."

Gesturing toward the back wall, he added, "It also has French doors that open onto the pool area. It's a much more dramatic entrance than simply using the door in the kitchen."

Megan just nodded, feeling strange about being in his bedroom and anxious to move on.

"And that's it," he said, leading her back into the hall.

"What's that, a closet?" she asked, pointing at the last door on the hallway.

"The basement." He grimaced. "The only unsightly part of the house. There's really no need for you to go down there."

"Fine with me," she said, pretending to shudder. "I'm not a big fan of spiders."

They were retracing their steps, heading back to the kitchen, when Megan spotted still another closed door.

"What's in there?" she asked, stopping in front of it.

"My home office," he said. "It's the one place that's off limits. I don't mean to be rude, but the bottom line is that I keep it locked because I've got some pretty valuable stuff in there. If anyone ever got to my files or my computer, it would be a disaster. Not only would I be in big trouble; so would the company I work for."

"I completely understand how you feel," she said. "People have to be so careful these days. You just never know what could happen."

Still, Megan couldn't help wondering if he'd gone a bit overboard. She decided, in the end, that his compulsion about home security wasn't any of her business. Besides, she reminded herself, she was in no position to complain since John's commitment to his work was what was behind this chance to housesit.

"You might want to look over these instructions I typed up," he suggested once they were back in the kitchen. He pulled a plastic magnet off the refrigerator and handed her the four typed pages it was holding in place. "I wrote down which days the garbage is picked up, how to handle the recycling, Endora's vet's phone number, everything you might need.

"And I left a pad and pencil next to the kitchen phone," he added, gesturing toward the wall phone next to the refrigerator. "I'd appreciate it if you'd answer it and take messages. But I don't get a lot of calls. Telemarketers, mostly." Pulling a cell phone out of his pants pocket, he added, "Frankly, I don't know how any of us survived before we had these."

"I'm glad everything's spelled out," Megan said, glancing through the sheaf of papers. "Did you leave an address where I should forward your mail?"

"I've arranged for the post office to forward it," he said. "And you can tell anyone who's trying to get in touch that my cell number is the best way to reach me.

"And of course you can call me any time," he added. "With questions, I mean. My number's on the first page."

"Just as long as I keep the time difference in mind," she said teasingly. "I don't want to wake you up in the middle of the night by calling to ask where the extra toilet paper is."

"Speaking of which, you're welcome to use anything here. Make yourself at home." John shrugged. "I guess that's it. You're welcome to show up any time in the afternoon the day after tomorrow and move your stuff in. By then, I'll be far, far away."

"In cold Minneapolis," she joked.

"In cold Minneapolis," he agreed. He reached into his pocket and pulled out a key.

"From Thursday noon on," he said as he handed it over, "I hope you'll consider the place yours."

As Megan headed down the front walkway, she was already planning her packing strategy. But she was suddenly distracted by the same feeling she'd had earlier: that someone was watching her.

Sure enough, a young man was standing at the end of the driveway, a few feet away from her car. Mid- to late-twenties, probably only a few years younger than she was. Even so, he had the look of a teenager who'd recently grown into a man's body, yet still hadn't fully made the adjustment.

His narrow shoulders and whisper-thin frame made him look as if a strong wind could blow him away. His skin was oddly pale, a dramatic contrast to his dark hair. He struck her as one of those rare southern Californians who avoided the sun.

Even more incongruous was the small white dog at the end of the leash he was clutching. She assumed it wasn't his, not only because it was a fluffy lap dog but even more because of its pink leash and matching rhinestone-studded collar. He kept yanking the leash, as if he found simply being in the dog's presence an irritation.

But it was his gray eyes she focused on. Even though they were shielded by thick glasses with black plastic frames, she immediately saw that they appeared to be drinking her in with unabashed greediness.

It was a look she knew well, one she'd seen in men's eyes ever since she'd stopped being a skinny kid who was all freckles and elbows. But unlike most of her friends, who basked in the power that came along with being an attractive young woman, that look had always made her uncomfortable.

She wasn't about to let some stranger have that effect on her.

"Hello," she said confidently, looking straight at him.

"Hi," he said, his hand jerking upward in an awkward wave. "I haven't seen you around here before."

"That's probably because I haven't been here before."

"My name's Russell." When she didn't reply, he asked, "What's yours?"

"Megan," she told him reluctantly.

"That's a nice name." He blinked a few times, opening and shutting his eyes with too much force, as if the gesture was more of a facial tic than a natural movement. "I live right over there."

He pointed at one of the more impressive mansions on the block. "See that blue house? That's mine. Well, my parents'. We moved here a couple of years ago."

"This looks like a great neighborhood." Turning toward the house, she added, "Well, it was nice—"

"I'm still living with them because I'm in school," he said, taking a step closer. "I'm taking two classes at Pasadena City College."

Suddenly the little white dog started barking. More of a yap, actually, an annoying high-pitched sound that was directed at something in the bushes she couldn't see.

Russell gave the dog another yank, so hard that it yelped. "Quiet, Jewel!" he hissed. "You stupid, disgusting little dog!"

Abruptly he turned his attention back to her, all smiles. "Anyway, it was really great meeting you. I hope I see you around again."

Megan forced a smile, thinking, Not if I can help it.

As she got back into her car, she expected to forget all about her new neighbor. Then felt an uncomfortable tightness in her stomach when she checked the rearview mirror and saw Russell standing in the same spot, his eyes fixed on her car as she drove away.

CHAPTER 3

S*he's the one*, he thinks happily. Megan. Pretty name, pretty girl. He watches as she drives away, keeping his eyes fixed on her car until it disappears from view.

A feeling of joy surging through him.

She's so nice. So considerate. So polite.

In fact, she's everything anyone could ever want.

Even though they just met, he already has a sense of who she is.

Of how she'll fit into the rest of his life.

A sense that she's the one he's been waiting for. The one he's been hoping for.

Simply picturing her in his mind fills him with joy.

He can't imagine anything better than finding someone like her. Someone who's so right for him.

Someone who's perfect for living happily ever after.

Now all he has to do is make her see things the same way.

Chapter 4

Home, sweet home, Megan thought happily. She stood in the middle of John's living room early on Thursday afternoon, hugging a cardboard carton of books and CDs. Looking around and smiling as Endora rubbed against her leg, purring.

She felt a great sense of relief over being in a brand new place, alone. The fact that hardly anyone knew where she was staying was turning out to provide her with a bonus: making her feel totally free. It was as if she'd dropped out of the world for a while. And she didn't have to drop back in until she was ready.

She drank in her new home, still marveling over how lucky she was. Her eyes traveled over the huge flat-screen TV, the Bose speakers, the impressive collection of CDs neatly lined up on the wall unit. James Taylor, Dave Matthews, Beyoncé, even Lady Gaga.

An interesting mix, she thought, amused. Especially for a single man.

Next she surveyed John's DVD collection, noting that it included both *Sleepless in Seattle* and *It's a Wonderful Life*, two of her all-time favorites.

She set the box down on the coffee table, suddenly hesitant. She realized she didn't quite know how to go about unpacking. After all, this was a temporary situation, and despite John's insistence that she make herself at home, she didn't know how long she would be here.

After a moment, she decided to follow his directive, but to keep her things separate. That way, when it was time to leave, she wouldn't have trouble disentangling hers from his.

She put the carton down on the coffee table, figuring she'd deal with the books and CDs she'd brought later. Instead, she headed into the bedroom, leaving Endora behind to stretch out contentedly in a patch of sunlight.

She had to admit that it felt a bit odd, staying in John's room. The guestroom would have been comfortable enough, and it didn't have much in the way of personal possessions in it. Still, as he'd noted, the master bedroom was the nicest room in the house.

She went inside, passing the large suitcase she'd deposited there earlier, and sat down on the bed. She found it amazingly comfortable.

Probably one of those super-expensive mattresses, she thought. The kind that's advertised on the radio all the time—the kind most people will never come even close to being able to afford.

Next she walked over to the French doors. Hanging over them were white curtains, the fabric so sheer she suspected they didn't do a very good job of blocking out the sun's rays.

Still, she welcomed the warmth on her face as she unlatched the doors and pulled them open. It was a glorious day, and the pool area looked like a photograph in an upscale home and garden magazine. Grass that was startlingly green edged the stone walkway encircling the pool, a large blue rectangle with a low diving board. In one corner of the yard stood two tremendous palm trees, their arched trunks mirroring each other. In the other corner was a rock garden that was meant to look rustic but that had undoubtedly been built by professionals. The entire space was enclosed by a wooden stockade fence that felt protective rather than oppressive.

I sure hit the jackpot, she thought giddily.

Next to the pool, she spotted a small white wrought-iron table with two chairs. Not exactly the ultimate in comfort, but the perfect place to set up her laptop and do some writing each day. There was even an umbrella, made of thick yellow canvas that she suspected would keep the sun from becoming an annoyance.

But first, she decided, I have to get serious about unpacking. Then this place will really feel like it's mine.

Leaving the French doors wide open, she retreated back into the house. She unlatched her suitcase, then started to slide the closet door to one side. She stopped, once again struck by the oddness of the situation.

How strange to be superimposing my things over someone else's, she mused. The two of us living in the same house, but at different times . . . eating off the same plates, sitting in the same chairs, studying our reflections in the same mirrors, but our lives never actually overlapping.

She turned and looked around the room once again, only this time in a different way. She noted that while John seemed to have put most of his things away to clear space for hers, the few things that were still on display gave her a better idea of who he really was. The turquoise plastic clock next to the bed, for example, with irregular angles that gave it the distinctive space-age look she knew had been popular in the 1950s. It looked like a find snatched up at a garage sale. Totally consistent with his love of classic TV shows, she decided, pleased by this whimsical touch.

The enlarged black and white photos dotting the pale blue walls also spoke to John's apparent interest in the past. Above the bed hung an aerial shot of Los Angeles back before the freeways were built, the landscape lush with palm trees that far outnumbered the stucco bungalows scattered across the hills. In another photo, right next to it, she recognized the Farmer's Market off Fairfax. But it had clearly been taken when the famous landmark consisted only of food stalls, long before a glitzy shopping center and a couple of characterless strip malls rose up around it.

She turned back to the closet, reminding herself that while she still felt uncomfortable poking around someone else's private space, there was no other way for her to find a place for her own things. Besides, John had told her to make herself at home.

"Wow! Thanks, John!" she cried aloud when she saw that he had freed up a good two feet of closet space for her things. While he'd probably taken a lot of his clothes to Minneapolis, leaving more than a dozen bare hangers behind, he'd pushed the shirts and jackets that remained to one side. He'd done the same with his shoes, condensing his collection to leave plenty of room for hers.

Megan half hummed, half sang an old Eagles tune as she hung up the clothes she'd brought. Next she arranged her shoes: a second pair of sandals, rubber flip-flops, and her shiny black heels.

She went over to the dresser and, experiencing that same eerie feeling that she was prying, slowly opened the top drawer. She was relieved to find that it was empty. With the same tentativeness, she opened the drawer below it. That one was empty too.

But when she pulled the handles of a third, she found that it was still packed tightly with John's clothes. Two piles of carefully folded sweaters, along with a polar fleece vest. The fourth drawer, just below, contained polo shirts and T-shirts. Subdued colors, mostly, neatly stacked up. Only one was slightly askew, probably because it was on the very bottom. The knit fabric was pale green, the color so out of line with the others that she suspected it was a gift from someone who hadn't known his taste.

Emboldened, she opened one drawer after another. She told herself she needed to see if he'd left her any more storage space, but she was actually finding that snooping around someone else's things was surprisingly interesting. The same meticulousness was exhibited in every drawer. Each one was filled with only one or two types of clothing—socks in one, shorts in another—every article folded, stacked, and lined up.

She began pulling her things out of the suitcase and putting them away. At first, she was tempted to copy John's organizational skills. But she quickly tired of folding her underpants and trying to stack her bras. In the end, she simply tossed everything into the two empty drawers.

Next she gathered up her cosmetics bag, shampoo, and other personal items she'd thrown into her suitcase. She carried them into the bathroom leading off the master bedroom.

"Whoa!" she exclaimed when she walked in and switched on the light.

When John had given her the tour of the house, they hadn't come in here. Through the open door, she hadn't been able to see anything besides the sand-colored tiles on the floor and the walls. Now, she could see just how luxurious it was. Not only did the tile in the good-sized room look expensive; the towels were huge and made of the softest cotton she had ever felt. It was outfitted with not one but two sinks. And in the back corner, there was a separate shower stall, its two outer walls made of glass.

But the high point was the bathtub. Not only was it Jacuzzi-style, with eight spigots dotting the beige porcelain surface, it was easily big enough for two.

A wave of sadness descended on Megan as she realized that the very first thought that had popped into her head was that she and Greg could have had a blast in it.

She shook her head. You can enjoy this gorgeous bathtub all by yourself, she thought. You can fill it with bubbles and light candles and even pour yourself a glass of champagne. This is your chance to enjoy the good life. And you deserve it.

She turned to one of the sinks and started arranging her things on the counter. But she paused and instead slid open the mirrored door of the medicine cabinet.

She wasn't surprised that John had cleared off the bottom shelf for her. One by one she lined up her personal items, singing softly to herself again. Deodorant, makeup, a half-empty tube of toothpaste. There was even room for her various pills, all stored in good-sized plastic bottles: Advil, Midol, and an assortment of vitamins that the manager of a health food store in Venice Beach had convinced her she simply couldn't live without.

As she slid the medicine cabinet closed, she caught sight of her reflection in the mirror. She decided she looked like someone who was slightly overwhelmed by moving day, noting that her cheeks were flushed and her skin was shiny with perspiration. She tucked a stray strand of dark brown hair behind her ear, one of many that had fallen away from the clip that was holding up the rest in a haphazard fashion.

She stopped mid-song when she noticed three drawers in the vanity. While the empty shelf had afforded her plenty of room for her own cosmetics, she couldn't resist peeking inside.

Once again, she was amazed by how much she was able to learn about the owner of the house. Thanks to the collection of boxes, tubes, jars, and bottles, she now knew that the list of ailments he'd struggled with in the recent past had included allergies, hemorrhoids, indigestion, and a cough severe enough to require a prescription for codeine-infused syrup. Sore muscles, too, at least if the old-fashioned hot-water bottle in the drawer was any indication. There were a few plastic vials as well, the kind used for prescription drugs, but she hesitated before examining them.

This is really none of your business, she told herself.

But she began pulling the orange vials out, one at a time, and reading the labels. Cipro, a powerful antibiotic. Singulaire, for allergies. A third plastic vial was nearly filled with round white pills labeled prednisone, which she remembered her roommate taking for mono in her freshman year.

So much for stumbling upon some deep dark pharmacological secret, she thought dryly, closing the drawer. No party drugs like OxyContin, no heavy-duty medications that indicated some exotic illness John struggles to keep from the rest of the world. As for his less interesting ailments, they must have been cured or he wouldn't have left these medications behind.

She was about to move on to another drawer when she remembered that she left groceries in the backseat of her car. She'd jammed on the brakes when she'd spotted a Trader Joe's on her way over, realizing the cupboard at her new home was likely to be bare. She'd taken her time going up and down the aisles, stocking up on all her favorites. Basics like milk and eggs and a hunk of cheddar cheese, but also two cartons of butternut squash soup, half a dozen cartons of yogurt, and a bag of gingersnaps.

She abruptly abandoned her exploration of John's bathroom and headed out to her car. As she leaned inside, gathering up the two grocery bags on the backseat floor, she heard someone call, "Hey, Megan!"

She stood upright, hugging a bag in each arm, her heart sinking as she turned and saw Russell standing at the end of the driveway. The same fluffy white dog stood next at him, its tense little body jerking impatiently every few seconds.

Megan glanced down self-consciously, suddenly aware that the red tank top she was wearing was tight and low-cut, that the white shorts she'd put on for moving day were so short that she rarely wore them out in public.

"Remember me?" he asked, his face lighting up expectantly.

"Of course I remember you." Her voice flat, she added, "Hello, Russell."

Beaming, he asked, "Need any help with those?" As he stepped closer, he gave the dog a hard yank.

Glancing down at her bags of groceries, she replied, "Thanks, but I'm fine. These aren't very heavy."

"I've been watching you," Russell said. "What I mean is, I saw that you're bringing boxes and suitcases inside. Are you moving in?"

She hesitated. "Yes and no."

He did the same blinking thing she'd noticed last time. "What does that mean?"

"This house still belongs to John Davis," she explained, trying to sound a little friendlier. "But I'm going to be taking care of it for a while."

His response was a look of confusion.

"I'm housesitting," she said. "John had to go away because of his job, and he needed somebody to take care of his house. I'm just staying here until he gets back."

"All alone?" he asked.

"What's wrong with that?"

"Nothing," he stuttered. "I mean, it's just that it's so big." Quickly he added, "But it's a nice house."

"It's a *great* house," Megan replied. She couldn't resist adding, "I love it already. The gardens, too. All these flowers are gorgeous."

Suddenly Russell brightened. "Let me know if you need any help with anything," he said. "Carrying stuff or unpacking or even finding your way around Pasadena. I don't have anything going on right now, so if you want me to do something for you—anything at all—I'd be happy to."

The idea of Russell becoming a regular presence in her life set Megan's teeth on edge. Resorting to the first excuse that popped into her head, she said, "Thanks, but I really shouldn't have people over. Since it's not actually my house and all."

Glancing down at the groceries, she pointedly said, "Well, I'd better get these inside."

"Okay, Megan!" Russell said with the same awkward wave. "See you soon!"

As she neared the front door, Megan turned just enough to see that he was still standing at the edge of the driveway. She hurried inside, making a point of locking the door behind her.

CHAPTER 5

O nce she was back inside the house, Megan was on edge as she bustled around the kitchen, putting her groceries away. It wasn't just the creepy guy who lived down the street, either, she realized. She was back to obsessing about the peculiarity of her situation—moving into a strange house, acting as if it was hers. Despite her attempts at convincing herself that she was lucky to be living in a house as nice as John's, simply being here was making her tense.

As she was putting away her milk and yogurt and other perishables, the abrupt clanking of the refrigerator's ice maker made her jump. A minute later, as she was lining up her other groceries on the counter, she froze when she suddenly heard a hissing sound.

"Is anyone there?" she instinctively called out.

It took her a few seconds to figure out it was only the sprinkler in the front yard.

She opened one of the lower cabinets, looking for a bowl for the fruit she'd bought, and a tarnished copper teakettle with a dent in the side tumbled out onto her foot.

"Ouch!" she cried, more startled than hurt. It was one more reminder that, unlike in a place that was really hers, she didn't know what she'd find behind a closed door.

Even Endora struck her as an eerie presence. The cat, lying in the corner of the kitchen, seemed to be watching her, studying her, in a way she found disconcerting. She remembered what John had said at Peet's about his cat appearing to possess special powers.

I don't belong here, Megan thought, as fearful and lonely as a kid who'd just been dropped off at summer camp for the first time. This is John's house, not mine.

She decided to make herself a cup of tea, thinking that its soothing warmth might calm her nerves. She found a box of Earl Grey teabags, then bypassed the old-fashioned teakettle and instead heated the water in the microwave.

Yet even that didn't help, she discovered as she stood leaning against the counter, sipping her tea and warily surveying her new surroundings. She downed less than half before dumping the rest into the sink and rinsing out the mug and spoon.

As she deposited them both on the drainboard, she told herself she was being ridiculous.

You'll get used to it, she thought. Of course it feels funny, finding yourself living all alone in such a big, unfamiliar place. Not only is everything new to you; none of this is really yours. It's only natural to feel a little discombobulated.

She suddenly remembered that the perfect antidote was only steps away.

Purposefully she went back to her bedroom and pulled a bathing suit out of the swirl of clothes in the drawer, a modest navy blue tank suit. But as soon as she kicked off her sandals, her cell phone trilled.

The fact that she nearly jumped out of her skin told her she hadn't quite gotten over her jitters. But her anxiety faded considerably when she checked caller ID and saw that her friend Brenda was calling.

"Hi, Brenda!" she answered. She couldn't remember the last time she was this happy to hear from anyone.

"Hey, girlfriend!" As usual, Brenda was bursting with exuberance. Megan was relieved that as usual, her enthusiasm was catching. "So what's this I hear about you moving out of Elissa's? She said something about you lucking out and inheriting a mansion in Pasadena."

Megan laughed. "I didn't inherit it. I'm just borrowing it for a while."

"How'd you manage that?"

"I'm housesitting," she explained. "This really nice guy who happens to live in a totally gorgeous house got sent to Minneapolis for a few weeks, and he needed somebody to take care of his cat while he was away."

"How'd you find him?"

"He put up an ad on the bulletin board at a copy shop in town. I called him and we met for coffee. I guess I passed inspection, because the next thing I knew he was handing me the keys."

"You mean he trusts a stranger with his house—and his cat?" Brenda exclaimed.

"I'm pretty responsible," Megan said, feeling a tad defensive. "Somehow, I managed to convince him of that."

"Well, I hope you can tear yourself away from the lap of luxury for a few hours this evening. I decided we need a girls' night out."

Megan recognized that a half hour earlier, she would have been reluctant to abandon what Brenda had so accurately described as the lap of luxury, even though she ordinarily loved going out with her friends. Yet now, given the uncharacteristic edginess that had unexpectedly descended upon her, she welcomed the distraction.

"Count me in," she said. "I assume Elissa and Chloe are both coming?"

"Yup. We're meeting at Acapulco at seven. You know, the one on Colorado."

"I'm so there," Megan said.

"Excellent. *Ciao!*"

When Megan hung up, she found that her anxiety over her new living situation had vanished. In fact, she could hardly wait to get outside to the house's main attraction.

She slithered into her tank suit, then checked her reflection in the mirror hanging above the dresser. She was pleased that she was still as fit as she was when she first bought this swimsuit. Then she pulled her hair back into a ponytail, opened the French doors, and stepped outside.

As she strode across the patio, the sun warmed her face and shoulders, its strength compensating for the coolness in the air. When she reached the edge of the pool, she dipped her foot in, pleased to find that just as John had promised, it was warm enough to swim.

She walked to the deep end, stepped onto the diving board, and jumped in. The sensation of being submerged reminded her of the deliciousness of sliding between crisp, clean sheets.

She felt at home.

Her arms and legs immediately began to move in a familiar rhythm, propelling her through the water with ease. She could feel the strength of her muscles, the power of her arms and her thighs. Stroke after stroke, a motion that was as familiar to her as breathing.

Yet something was off. Nagging at her, pushing its way forward from the back of her mind.

Of course she knew what it was. Ellie drowning.

It's because you just told John about it, she told herself. Dredging it all up again, reliving something you'd rather forget.

Even so, forgetting was impossible. The memory of being in the water with her cousin was still as crystal clear as it had ever been: the two of them splashing around together on that hot summer day, no more than thirty feet from shore. The waves calm, the water not terribly deep—just a few inches above their heads. Both of them veterans of swimming lessons, as comfortable in the water as two little fishes.

Yet one minute Ellie was beside her, bubbling around in the waves, and the next minute, she was dead.

Just as clearly, Megan remembered the feelings of guilt that gripped her afterward. All the therapy sessions that had followed. The suffocating attention of her parents, the unremitting scrutiny of the doctors and all the other professionals who were so committed to seeing her heal. How she'd hated being the focus of all that attention. The feeling that despite their kind eyes, their soft-spoken words, somehow they blamed her.

She forced herself to put it out of her mind.

Concentrate on the water, she commanded herself. Think about swimming. Nothing else.

Megan did one lap after another for nearly half an hour. Finally letting go of the ugly memories, finally easing into what came to her as naturally as walking. Surprising herself by how much she had missed this.

She came back into the house, into the bathroom, promising herself she would make time to swim every day. At least once. As she turned on the shower, she was completely focused on how fortunate she was. She silently thanked John— for having a cat, for having such a wonderful pool, for being sent to Minneapolis, all so she could have this place to herself.

Megan's hair was still wet as she pulled on jeans and a T-shirt and headed into the backyard again, this time with her laptop. Sitting at the table, under the big yellow umbrella, she checked her email. She was pleased to see a few messages from friends she'd made at work, people she was afraid wouldn't bother to keep in touch with her. Next she looked up the weather for the next few days and checked her credit card balance.

Then she clicked on Word and opened a short story she'd started working on the week before. Hunching over her laptop, she fiddled with the first few paragraphs. But it was slow going, and she was frustrated by her inability to make any real progress.

It wasn't until she'd abandoned the story and opened a blank page that she was finally able to lose herself. Before long, her fingers tap-danced across the keyboard. She'd been keeping a journal for as long as she could remember, not only recording what she'd done that day but even more importantly writing about whatever came into her mind.

Today, she found her rhythm quickly. Yet while she began by writing about the house she'd just moved into, before long she was involved in a one-person therapy session. Her disappointment in Greg, her anger at herself for being roped in by him in the first place, her apprehensions about this new, still-unformed chapter of her life . . . it all spilled out, her fingers clicking keys with lightning speed.

It wasn't until a shadow drifted across the keyboard that she realized how late it had gotten. Checking the time at the bottom of the screen, she saw that she needed to get ready for her night out. Reluctantly she shut down her laptop and dragged herself back inside the house.

As she got ready, leaning over the sink to brush on L'Oreal blush in a shade called Subtle Sable, she realized that slowly but surely, she was starting to get used to her new digs. This time, she wasn't the least bit thrown by the unexpected gurgle of the pool filter turning on. In fact, she was suddenly ambivalent about going out on her first evening here, part of her wishing she could stay in and enjoy the solitude of this magnificent house that had suddenly become hers.

But she hadn't forgotten that not long ago, she'd been overcome with loneliness. She also knew how much she enjoyed the company of her three closest friends, who she now feared she might have given short shrift during the time she was so enthralled with Greg.

So she stood in front of the open closet, trying to decide what to wear. Tonight definitely called for something short and flirty and fun. She chose a sleeveless silk dress splashed with pink flowers. A bit dressy, maybe, but she decided her housesitting gig called for a celebration.

She stepped out of her jeans and pulled off her T-shirt, then slipped on the dress, relishing the feeling of the satiny fabric caressing her skin. Next she slipped on her favorite shoes, the shiny black ones. As she anticipated, the three-inch heels instantly made her feel elegant.

Before leaving, Megan ran through a mental checklist, determined to be as responsible as she'd promised John she'd be. Feed Endora, check. Refill her water bowl, check. Make sure appliances and unnecessary lights are off, check. Test the back door to make sure it's firmly shut, check.

She went into the living room, where she switched on the porch light. After hesitating for a moment, she turned on the lamp next to the couch, as well.

As she stepped out onto the front porch, the image of Russell loitering at the end of the driveway flashed through her mind. Before heading out for the night, she checked the front door, wanting to be doubly-sure she'd remembered to lock it.

CHAPTER 6

H e stands across the street, his hands in his pockets. Trying to adopt a casual pose even though he's hidden by the darkness. His eyes glued to the front of 55 Sierra. Watching. Just watching.

No sign of movement, at least not yet. But he can wait.

He's come prepared, putting on dark clothes, even bringing along a bottle of water.

Time seems to have come to a standstill. All around him, the night is silent. There are no signs of life on this isolated cul-de-sac.

Not that he minds waiting. Not at all.

Having Megan all to himself is worth whatever it takes.

Suddenly, movement.

His heartbeat speeds up as the front door opens and she appears in the doorway.

He can tell by the way she's dressed that she's going out. Partying, he thinks, frowning. Or going out to a bar.

He studies her from a hundred yards away, noting the short dress that swirls around her knees, the high heels, the makeup.

His face tenses into a scowl.

He steps further back into the shadows, not wanting to be spotted. Still watching as she skips along the front walkway to her car. As she climbs into the front seat, her dress rides up, just a little, revealing a patch of thigh.

He swallows, noticing how dry his mouth has become. He takes a swig of water.

But his eyes remain focused on her.

He watches her car back out of the driveway, maneuvering the cul-de-sac with ease. He steps behind a tree as she drives past. But it's already too dark for her to see him. If she even takes the time to glance in his direction.

He wonders, for a moment, if he should follow her. After all, he wants to know everything about her.

No, he decides. There's plenty of time for that. Besides, he has a better plan in mind for tonight.

Something bigger. Considerably more daring.

And infinitely more satisfying.

CHAPTER 7

The Mexican chain restaurant Brenda had chosen, Acapulco, was only a ten-minute drive from John's. Since the members of their foursome were fairly far flung, living in different parts of the sprawling city-without-a-center, they got together in different neighborhoods. With both Megan and Elissa living in Pasadena at the moment, meeting for dinner at the East Colorado Boulevard eatery had made sense.

Not only did they all live in different parts of the city, they all had distinctly different personalities. But their unlikely grouping only added to the fun. They played off each other in a way that worked amazingly well.

Brenda, a physician's assistant at the OB/GYN practice Megan had started going to, was known for her outspokenness. Elissa, the former college roommate of one of her friends back east who'd put them in touch, was considerably quieter. Her even temperament made her well suited for her job as an administrator at Caltech—the California Institute of Technology. It had also made her a fairly compatible roommate, at least for as long as that lasted.

Chloe was the glamorous one. With her long, silky blond hair and startlingly blue eyes, it was no surprise that she was an aspiring actress. And like so many of the beautiful young women who flocked to L.A. from all corners of the globe, she supported her ambitions by working at jobs that didn't interfere with auditions. They'd become friends when she'd been waiting tables in a coffee shop that Megan frequented while she still worked at Hayworth.

The four women had met at this restaurant a couple of times before, attracted as much by the party atmosphere created by the brightly-colored walls and piped in mariachi music as they were by the sweet, icy margaritas served in fishbowl sized glasses.

As Megan approached their table, she saw she was the last to arrive.

"Here she is!" Brenda squealed. Her bold personality was accompanied by a strong physical presence: a cloud of wildly curly brown hair, a large, plump frame, and a fondness for brightly colored clothing and clunky costume jewelry.

This evening, she was draped in a hot-pink silk tunic and flowing purple silk pants, with a string of black beads the size of golf balls perched on her chest. "We went ahead and ordered you a margarita. I figured if you didn't want it for some insane reason, I'd do you the favor of drinking it."

Elissa scooched over to make room for her on the wooden bench. Unlike Brenda, she favored earth tones that helped her blend in with her surroundings and wore her fine, light brown hair in a short, practical style. "We ordered the nachos, too. We're all starving."

Chloe grimaced. "Would you at least give the poor girl a chance to sit down?"

Megan slid in next to Elissa, grinned at the other three, and let out a deep sigh.

"This has been such a crazy week," she said, rolling her eyes and laughing.

"So we hear," Brenda commented. "But crazy in a *good* way, right?"

Before Megan had a chance to respond, Brenda said, "Ah, here's our hunky waiter. The only thing more delicious-looking than he is are those four margaritas he's got on his tray."

As the drinks were passed around, Brenda continued to half-whisper comments about the waiter's good looks. Megan hoped his English was as bad as he pretended.

But once they'd finished their toast—"To margaritas!"—and everyone had sipped the sugary lemon-lime concoction, the focus was back on her.

"It's awesome," Megan said with a little shrug. "I can't believe how lucky I am."

A vision of her new neighbor, the creepy kid from down the street, flashed into her mind, but she immediately brushed it away. With her friends playing the role of an enraptured audience, she couldn't resist the urge to brag.

"The house is absolutely gorgeous," she continued. "It's here in Pasadena, on a beautiful, quiet street. A cul-de-sac, actually, so it's really quiet. It's beautifully decorated, and there's a pool—"

"A pool!" Chloe squealed.

"It's solar-heated," Megan added. "I actually used it this afternoon."

"Now you can start swimming again!" Elissa exclaimed. "I remember you telling me once about how important it's been in your life."

"Swimming?" Brenda asked, looking confused. "What am I missing?"

"Megan swam competitively in college," Elissa said, proudly adding, "It just so happens that our friend here is a swimming *star*."

Chloe's eyes widened. "I had no idea! Megan, you never said a word about that. You're way too modest!"

Megan shrugged. "I guess I was pretty good, but competing was never the most important thing for me. Swimming is just something I happen to love."

"In that case," Chloe said, "it really is wonderful that you've got your own swimming pool." Teasingly, she added, "So when are we invited over?"

"Can I bring my husband?" Brenda asked. "And my kid?"

"I doubt that the homeowner wants his housesitter throwing pool parties," Elissa said, lifting her glass by the stem.

"Hey, what he doesn't know won't hurt him," Brenda countered, her dark eyes shining. "But forget the pool. Tell us about the guy who owns the house!"

"There's not much to tell," Megan replied.

"Don't tell me: he's married," Chloe said.

"Nope," Megan said. "Not married. Not even divorced—even though he's at least forty."

Brenda frowned. "Not a good sign."

"Unless he's gay," Elissa interjected.

"I don't think so," Megan said. "I didn't get that vibe at all. But he's kind of . . ." She wrinkled her nose. "Nerdy."

"Nothing wrong with that," Brenda insisted. "You've got what it takes to loosen up a nerdy guy, Megan."

"Besides," Elissa added, "maybe he just seems that way because he's a bit older than you. But there's a lot to be said for older men. They're more mature, they appreciate the fact that you're young and gorgeous . . ."

"Don't forget money," Chloe added mischievously. "They're pretty well-established in their careers by forty."

"Then there's real estate!" Brenda chirped. "The guy has a big house with a pool, right? That's not too shabby."

"There's only one major problem," Megan said dryly. "Even if I was inclined toward romance, it'd be kind of difficult since the guy is fifteen hundred miles away. In Minneapolis, of all places."

"There are such things as airplanes," Elissa pointed out.

"And cell phones," Chloe added, nodding knowingly.

"Besides, he's not going to be in Minneapolis forever, right?" Brenda said. "It's not like he's moving there. Otherwise, he would have sold this gorgeous house of his and you wouldn't be living in it."

"There's nothing wrong with considering all your options," Chloe said. "Especially now that Greg is out of the picture."

"Speaking of Greg," Elissa said, her voice suddenly strained. She fixed her eyes on the plastic stirrer she was moving around in circles in the margarita foam. "He called me yesterday, looking for you."

"Really." Megan was aware that silence had instantly fallen over the table. "What did he want?"

"He didn't say," Elissa replied. "I hope you don't mind, but I told him you'd gotten a housesitting gig and that you were moving in today. I figured I had to explain why you weren't staying with me anymore.

"Besides," she added, "I couldn't resist making it sound as if you were really living it up. I told him you were staying in a mansion near the Huntington Gardens."

"Good," Chloe said with a firm nod of her head. "Let that jerk know she's doing great without him."

"I agree," Brenda seconded. "Good riddance to bad rubbish. Megan, you're way too good for him."

"Thanks, you guys," Megan said. She bent her head and sipped her margarita, not wanting her friends to see that their show of support was making her tear up.

"Personally, I think this guy John has potential," Chloe added. "Good career, nice house, and it sounds like he's into you."

"Why would you say that?" Megan asked, surprised.

"He left his house, his cat, and his entire life in your hands!" Chloe replied. "He obviously trusts you!"

"Just because somebody trusts you to feed their cat doesn't mean they're destined to fall in love with you," Megan pointed out.

"Tell us more about him," Brenda demanded. "Have you done any snooping?"

Elissa nodded. "You could find out a lot about the guy by looking through all his stuff."

"I'm not going to look through his stuff!" Megan exclaimed. Thoughtfully, she added, "Although I did have to open a few drawers to find places to put my things."

"What did you find?" Chloe asked eagerly.

"Nothing too interesting, I'm afraid. Just that he's got allergies and that he keeps his shirts and sweaters nicely folded." Grimacing, Megan added, "In fact, he's kind of a neat freak."

"Nothing wrong with that," Chloe commented.

"If I were you, I'd dig a little deeper," Brenda said.

Megan rolled her eyes. "Maybe you're interested in whether the guy wears boxer shorts or briefs, but I'm not. For now, I just want the chance to enjoy his house and his pool—and to be alone for a while."

"Still, you'd better be ready to strike once he's back in town." Brenda swept her glass through the air. "You know there aren't that many guys around with potential."

"That's the truth," Megan agreed.

"How do you feel about living alone?" Chloe asked her. "As someone with three roommates, to me it sounds like a dream come true."

"I don't know," Megan admitted. "I only moved into the house today. I haven't even slept there yet."

"I remember when I first got my own apartment," Elissa said thoughtfully. "The first few nights were surprisingly tough. I kept hearing noises and freaking out. It took me a while to figure out that they were nothing at all, just the building settling or the refrigerator motor coming on or something silly like that. Living all by yourself definitely takes some getting used to."

Megan nodded, comforted by the knowledge that she wasn't the only one to find living alone an adjustment. "I've experienced that kind of thing already. It is kind of strange, being all alone in a big, empty house."

"Especially since it belongs to someone else," Brenda noted. "The homeowner has all his stuff around, right? I'd think that would feel kind of weird."

"Our Megan is tough," Chloe insisted. "She'll get used to it. Besides, I wish I had the problem of trying to adjust to living in a mansion. With a luxurious pool, no less, all to herself."

"Speaking of which," Megan said, "I can't imagine that John would mind if you all came over to use the pool. What's everybody's schedule look like?"

BlackBerries and iPhones were whipped out, calendars were consulted. They finally determined that miraculously, Sunday afternoon, only three days away, worked for all of them. Megan gave them the address and directions.

"I'm so glad I have something to look forward to this weekend," Chloe said, tucking her BlackBerry back into her purse. "Which reminds me: did I tell you that last weekend I finally went out with that accountant I met at my friend Nicole's dinner party?"

As the conversation shifted to Chloe's catastrophic dinner with a man whose main passion in life turned out to be bird-watching, Megan was still thinking about John—and how little she actually knew about him. In fact, there was something unsettling about how quick her friends were to see a man who was a total mystery to her as a possible replacement for Greg.

They're only teasing, she thought, sipping her drink. And you're being too sensitive.

As her friends' animated conversation tumbled down around her like a waterfall, she told herself she was still recovering from the fact that she and Greg weren't together anymore. She still needed more time to get used to the idea. Time, and solitude.

Fortunately, she now had plenty of both.

CHAPTER 8

Outside the house, he waits, still shielded by darkness. The longer he postpones going in, the more he prolongs the anticipation, the more excited he becomes. Adrenaline shoots through his veins, his palms grow damp, his nerves jangle as if he's being shot through with electricity.

Forcing himself to delay something he can hardly wait to do creates a longing that hovers between excruciating and pleasurable.

Three minutes, four minutes, five . . .

Part of the waiting is about playing it safe. Making sure she's not coming back to retrieve something she forgot.

Once he's decided enough time has gone by, he saunters toward the house, his hands jammed in his pockets. Acting as if absolutely nothing is out of the ordinary.

As if his heart isn't pounding wildly in his chest.

He circles around to the side, opening the metal gate slowly so it doesn't creak. The bushes and trees are equally dense here, all but concealing an outer door that leads to the basement. There's no walkway, either, just an uninviting dirt path that looks like an afterthought, rather than part of the landscaping design.

He's decided that using the basement door is the best way to get into the house, since anyone who happens by won't see him.

No one will come by, he tells himself. No one is watching. *I'm* the one doing the watching.

He climbs down the three concrete steps that lead to the door, then crouches down and picks up a big rock lying nearby. Despite the wild undergrowth, it sticks out like the proverbial sore thumb, since it's the only one of its kind. Underneath it he finds a key.

Not exactly the most creative hiding place, he thinks, his mouth twisting into a wry smile. But it sure makes things easy.

Once he gains entrance, he finds himself in a small, dark space.

He hates enclosed spaces.

But he doesn't linger. Instead, he heads up the stairs to the main floor, doing his best not to make any noise even though he knows there's no one here.

In the living room, he glances around, noting the ways in which she's already made herself at home. A sweater lies draped over the back of a chair. Books and CDs are strewn across the coffee table, the empty carton he suspects once contained them pushed into a corner. A CD case with a picture of Lady Gaga, looking as grotesque as usual, lying on the couch.

She's starting to act as if this place is hers.

He jumps as something moving in the dining room catches his eye.

Then lets out his breath when he sees it's only the flash of orange fur. He hears a loud meow as the cat pads toward him, seemingly happy to have some company.

He ignores the cat, instead going into the kitchen. He surveys the food neatly lined up, boxes and jars kept separate. Next he yanks open the refrigerator and sees a hunk of cheese and several cartons of yogurt stashed away.

He turns to face the counter and spots the drainboard next to the sink. On it are a spoon and a mug, which he surmises recently touched her lips.

While the bedroom is next on his list, he hesitates before leaving the kitchen. Not that he's having second thoughts about going in there. Instead, the prospect of entering her private space, the place where she'll sleep, undress, and do everything else that constitutes the most personal part of her life, is so titillating, so delicious, that he wants to savor it.

This is the first time, he thinks gleefully. Which means it will be the most thrilling.

And then he can't wait a moment more. He hurries in, impatient to see it all.

He begins with the closet. She's left the door open, and he plants himself in front of it.

Hanging on one side are her clothes. He leans forward and gathers three or four dresses in both hands, pressing his face into the fabric. Smelling her. Surrounding himself with her essence. As he does, he can feel the delicious tightness in his crotch.

He strokes the fabric of each garment hanging inside, relishing the different textures: the crispness of a blouse, the nubbiness of a sweater, the softness of a sundress. Then he crouches down and picks up her shoes, one by one. Holds them next to his cheek, breathing in the smell of the leather, stroking the hardness of the heels.

Reluctantly he abandons the closet, moving on to the dresser. A shockwave of delight runs through him when he finds that the top drawer is filled with panties and bras, jumbled together. The chaos frees him to pick up several items, the tightness growing even more excruciatingly wonderful as he does.

Silky thongs, pink and lavender and pale blue . . . those are his favorites. He strokes his cheek with the slippery fabric, then his neck. On impulse, he takes a pink pair and stuffs it into his pocket.

For later.

The bras are less intoxicating. There's something cold and mechanical about them. He touches a few, but decides he doesn't like them.

He closes the drawer and goes into the bathroom. He opens the medicine cabinet, noticing that just as she lined up her boxes of food in the kitchen, she has lined up her cosmetics and vitamins and toothpaste. He picks up each item, one at a time, running his fingers against the hard plastic cases, opening a few of the bottles and jars and sniffing what's inside.

He takes care to put them back in the same order. But once again, he can't help taking a souvenir, this time a gold tube of lipstick. He slips it into the same pocket.

He's tempted to linger, but has no way of knowing how long she'll be out.

He doesn't want to take any chances.

He takes one more look around the bedroom, making sure that nothing is disturbed, that everything remains exactly as she left it. Then turns, preparing to head back out the way he came in.

But he stops. On impulse, he decides to leave something behind.

After all, he reasons, I took some of her things. It's only fair that I leave her something in return.

He already knows what it will be. His heart races as he anticipates her reaction, the sheer joy she'll experience from knowing that someone is thinking of her.

He heads into the kitchen. Rifles through drawers until he finds what he's looking for.

A pair of scissors, shiny and sharp.

He clutches it in his hand, suddenly anxious to fulfill his mission. As he steps into the hallway, he sees the cat standing in his path, looking at him questioningly.

"You won't tell anyone I was in here, will you?" he asks.

Then smiles, knowing perfectly well that the cat is not about to give away his secret.

CHAPTER 9

While the drinks at Acapulco weren't particularly strong, downing three of them—at Brenda's insistence—had its effect. By the time Megan pulled into the driveway at 55 Sierra Avenue, her head was buzzing. She'd made a point of driving home on as many side streets as she could, aware that she wasn't in the best shape to be behind the wheel. She was relieved to be back, not only because she'd made it in one piece, but even more because now she could relish that delicious solitude she'd been craving. Her friends had decided to make an early night of it, which left her plenty of time to enjoy her new place before going to bed.

As she headed up the front walkway, she studied the house and the lush gardens that surrounded it, still trying to absorb the fact that she lived here now. The alcohol in her system made everything appear a little fuzzier than usual, as if she was looking at an Impressionist painting.

She'd nearly reached the front steps when she froze.

A flash of color, bright pink, lying right outside the door, had caught her eye.

Did I drop something on my way out? she wondered, as usual feeling that if something was wrong, she was responsible.

It wasn't until she'd taken a few steps closer that she understood what she was looking at: a bouquet of flowers, probably cut from one of the flowering shrubs in the front yard. The sight of it sent an unpleasant jolt through her, the disturbing feeling that arises from something being where it's not supposed to be.

What's wrong with this picture?

Russell, she thought with annoyance, scowling at the cluster of five or six blossoms that were already starting to look scraggly. *That weird guy who lives down the street. I was afraid he'd turn out to be a pain.*

She glanced around, then realized how silly she was to think he might be out there somewhere, waiting for her. Watching her, wanting to see her reaction.

With a sigh, she leaned over and scooped up the flowers. Her first impulse was to toss them onto the ground behind the bushes. But she didn't want him to spot them lying in the yard, discarded, if he came by again—which he undoubtedly would, sooner or later.

After all, while she certainly didn't want to encourage him, she also didn't want to appear rude. So she held onto them as she opened the front door with the key, already planning to toss them into the trash. That way, her overzealous neighbor would never know what she really thought of his gesture.

Megan was determined not to let this intrusion get in the way of enjoying her new home for the rest of the evening. Yet as soon as she stepped into the house, instead of feeling welcoming, it struck her as startlingly silent.

At least Endora was there, padding over to greet her as she closed the front door behind her, turning both the bolt and the lock in the doorknob.

"Hey, pussycat!" she cooed.

She crouched down and stroked her soft orange fur. Endora rubbed against her leg, purring appreciatively. "I bet you're glad I'm home. You don't like being alone, do you? That's something we have in common, but I'm trying to learn to embrace my freedom."

After a minute or two, Endora lost interest in being petted. Abruptly she turned and took off, trotting toward the back of house.

Leaving Megan alone again.

It's amazing how quiet this place seems, she thought, glancing around the living room.

It wasn't as if she'd never been all by herself in a house before, but there was something about being in someone else's home that kept it from feeling—well, homey. In fact, now that she was alone, the silence, the solitude, and the simple *strangeness* made her uncomfortable.

She decided to do something about the house's almost unbearable emptiness. She kicked off her shoes, deliberately leaving them in the middle of the rug. Then she headed for the CD player on the wall unit, grabbing John's Lady Gaga CD and loading it into the machine.

Loud music instantly filled the room. She turned the volume up even higher.

Even though the bouncy melody and the pulsing rhythm were completely out of sync with her surroundings, they instantly worked wonders. Swaying in time to the relentless disco beat, Megan pranced into the kitchen, where the first thing she did was toss the bedraggled flowers into the trash.

As she turned around, her eyes lit on the drainboard, where that afternoon she'd left the mug and spoon from her cup of tea to dry. Something seemed off.

It took her a few seconds to realize what it was. She always made a habit of placing cups and glasses upside down to make sure the insides would dry. In fact, it was one of those things she tended to be irrationally uptight about. But the mug was standing upright.

Now *that's* odd, she thought, turning it over so it was the way it was supposed to be. Maybe you're losing your mind.

Recognizing how hard on herself she was being, she thought, Or maybe you're still discombobulated because you're living in a new place, one that's not really yours.

With a sigh, she opened the refrigerator. Not much in there, but one thing caught her eye: the bottle of white wine she'd picked up at Trader Joe's. Not that she needed any more alcohol.

"Hey, you can do whatever you feel like doing!" she said aloud. "This is your house. This is your life. You can be as wild and crazy as you want!"

She grabbed the wine bottle, popped off the cork, and pulled a wine glass off the shelf. It was surprisingly heavy.

She was no expert, but she supposed it must be crystal. The good stuff.

Defiantly she filled her glass almost to the top.

She danced to the loud music, the tile floor cool beneath her bare feet. She paused only to drink some of her wine, gulping down a good inch to keep it from spilling.

But despite her attempts at acting like a devil-may-care party girl, she realized there was no joy in what she was doing. Even having Endora join her, or at least stand in the doorway watching her with grave curiosity, didn't help. She wondered why she wasn't having more fun.

The answer immediately came into focus, leaping out from the shadows at the back of her mind where it had been looming for weeks.

Greg. And the fact that he wasn't in her life anymore.

For the millionth time, she reminded herself that her decision to break up with him was for the best.

Why couldn't he have been just a little bit different? she wondered. Because, she thought disdainfully, answering her own question, then he wouldn't be Greg.

She picked up Endora and plopped onto one of the stools next to the island. Stroking the cat distractedly with one hand and leaning the other elbow on the cold granite, she thought back to their early days together. When she and Greg had first met while waiting for a table at a popular restaurant in Santa Monica, she'd experienced a euphoria she hadn't felt since she'd first hooked up with her college boyfriend—her one other major romance up to that point. It caused her to float through her days, energizing her, distracting her, turning her into a creature even she didn't recognize.

Whatever she did—brushing her teeth, sitting at her desk at work, even going out with her friends—she was thinking about him. Remembering the funny things he'd said the last time they'd spoken. Reliving the intoxicating sensation of him lightly brushing a strand of hair away from her cheek. Freezing with her toothbrush or her drink in midair as she replayed the last time she'd kissed him, feeling her mouth melt against his, relishing the feeling of the two of them practically becoming a single being.

The initial thrill had faded after the first few weeks. But it was replaced by something almost as wonderful: the security, the ease, of being with someone she felt completely comfortable with. Someone who finished her sentences, who didn't care that her hair needed washing, who didn't even blink when she reached over and plucked French fries off his plate.

But along with that increased familiarity came learning about someone's faults. And in Greg's case, his major fault happened to be a complete lack of ambition.

Not that he didn't *want* things, just that he wasn't willing to do what was required to get them. It was as if he expected that whatever he wanted would magically fall from the sky—or that someone else would take care of the hard parts for him.

He'd always been open about the fact that it had taken him six and a half years to get through college. In fact, it almost seemed to be something he was proud of. Then he drifted from job to job, insisting that it was smart for a person to spend their twenties trying to decide which career path to follow, rather than jumping right into something immediately after graduating.

The last straw had been Greg's interest in applying to graduate school in architecture. At least, she'd thought he was interested. After all, he'd been talking about becoming an architect since the first night they'd met. Famous architects and the buildings they designed was one of the many subjects he could talk about with authority.

He claimed it was something he'd been considering for quite a while, and was only now realizing that was the route he'd been meant to follow all along. He talked endlessly about his strong visual sense, insisting that at the same time he was also good at math and physics. Architecture, he was certain, was a field that had the potential to focus his varied interests once and for all.

Then, the first time they'd had dinner together after she'd learned she was being laid off, she asked him if he'd decided which architecture schools he was going to apply to.

"I've decided it's not for me," he'd replied with a shrug. "Not when I'd have to go back to school for three whole years!"

That was when she'd snapped. She realized that the person she'd been telling herself he was—the person who, on occasion, she'd envisioned possibly spending the rest of her life with—was nothing more than a construct of her own making.

All the doubts about him that had lingered at the back of her mind suddenly flared up with such clarity and strength that she could no longer rationalize them away. Her friends' warnings, which she'd attributed to them not knowing him as well as she did, rose up right beside them, just as impossible to ignore.

She'd known from the moment she told him it was over that she'd done the right thing. But that didn't mean it was easy.

Since she'd met Greg soon after moving to L.A., being here in this still-unfamiliar place sometimes filled her with an aching, terrifying loneliness. She felt as if she was being held under water, fighting forces she didn't have a chance of controlling.

She was so lost in thought that when her cell phone trilled, she picked it up without checking Caller ID. Her first thought was that it was John, calling to check up on her or even to chastise her, as if from halfway across the country he somehow knew she'd been partying just a little too hard.

When she heard Greg's familiar voice saying, "Hey, Megs! How's it going?" she reacted as if someone had just doused her with cold water.

"Greg?" she said, her shock reflected in her voice. She was so startled that she stopped petting Endora, who reacted by leaping off her lap.

"It's me, all right," he said, his cheerfulness sounding forced.

"Is everything okay?" she asked, puzzled about why he was calling. She kept the phone clasped against her ear as she darted back into the living room to turn down the music.

"Everything's great!" he insisted. "How about you?"

As she dropped onto the couch, her defenses were already snapping firmly into place. "Things are fine," she said guardedly.

"So I hear," he replied. "Elissa told me all about the amazing housesitting gig you landed."

"I really lucked out," she said, wishing Elissa hadn't told him anything at all. "So . . . things are going well?"

"Couldn't be better."

"That's good."

A heavy silence fell. She was about to tell him that she was in the middle of something important when he said, "I miss you, Megs."

She didn't reply, and he added, "I thought what we had together was amazing."

"Look, Greg. I don't think—"

"At the risk of sounding trite, I was hoping we could still be friends."

She gave his idea serious consideration. "I don't know," she finally said. "I'm not very good at that kind of thing."

"It just so happens that I'll be near Pasadena tomorrow night," he went on, as if he hasn't heard a word she'd said. "I'm going to a Lakers game with a few buddies, and I got roped into picking one of them up. He lives in Glendale, and since I'll be so close, I thought maybe I'd stop over to see this palace you're living in. Just for an hour or so."

Maybe it was being in a brand new place, all alone, or maybe it was that she really did want to show off how well she was doing without him. But before she could stop herself, she said, "I suppose that would be okay."

"Excellent," he said. "Tell you what: I'll even bring something to drink. A nice bottle of wine, maybe."

"Okay," she agreed, then couldn't resist adding, "We can sit outside by the pool."

"Your new place has a *pool?* I'm impressed. So I'll have to leave by seven to pick up Pete, but I can probably get to you by six."

"Six is good," she said. "I'll tell you how to get to the house."

"I have a pretty good idea where it is." Quickly, he added, "Elissa told me. You're near the Huntington Gardens, right?"

She gave him the address, along with directions.

As soon as she hung up, she started doubting her decision to allow Greg to invite himself over. But she was suddenly exhausted, too exhausted to agonize over whether she'd just made a huge mistake.

Her overwhelming fatigue was the result of too much alcohol, combined with the shock of hearing from the last person in the world she expected to invade her brand new space. She wanted nothing more than to go to bed.

"G'night, Endora," she called as she pulled herself off the couch and shuffled into her bedroom.

Her head felt as if it was coated in cotton batting. It was a relief to undress, pulling off the pink flowered dress and kicking off her shoes, aiming them in the direction of the closet. She retrieved the oversized T-shirt she liked to curl up in from the drawer and slipped it on, by that point positively craving sleep.

Without even bothering to brush her teeth, she made a beeline for the bed. She pulled back the sheet and dropped onto the mattress, once again marveling over how comfortable it was. And before she had a chance to think about much more, she was out for the night.

CHAPTER 10

What have I done? It was the first cohesive thought that formed in Megan's head the next morning. The simple sentence catapulted her back into consciousness, a place where she immediately realized she'd rather not be.

"Ugh!" she groaned.

The mere act of uttering the single syllable made her head throb. She realized it was the result of more than regret. Consuming too much tequila and wine was another factor.

She yanked the covers over her head, but felt something weighing down the blankets, just a bit. Before she could figure out what it could possibly be, four little hammers pounded across her thighs and onto her stomach.

Endora. Her soft, furry face was suddenly up against Megan's. She let out a loud *meow*. Reminding her there was a reason she was here in John's house, that she had someone to take care of aside from herself.

Groaning loudly, Megan dragged herself out of bed, deciding she'd worry about Greg resurfacing later. Moving around the house required her to open her eyes, and she squinted in the early morning sunlight that insisted on pushing its way through the flimsy curtains covering the French doors.

As she plodded into the kitchen, Megan suddenly felt overwhelmed by being in a new place. Simply making herself breakfast today was going to be a challenge, something she'd rather not have to grapple with, given the sorry state of both her head and her mood.

Making coffee, for example. She pawed through every cabinet, looking for filters, finally finding them hidden behind a canister of flour. Then she wrestled with the coffeepot, trying to figure out how to open the basket.

Endora watched her every move, meowing crossly.

"All right, all right, I hear you," Megan muttered. "Coffee first, cat food second. That's the rule."

She finally got the coffeepot going. Encouraged by its happy burbling, and even more so by the smell of fresh coffee wafting through the kitchen, she turned her attention to her charge.

The sound of hard pellets of dry cat food spilling into a ceramic bowl sent Endora into a state of ecstasy. Once the cat had been fed, Megan succeeded in cajoling the mysterious toaster oven into turning an English muffin brown.

Two cups of coffee and a slightly underdone muffin worked wonders. By the time she rinsed out her mug, she was already planning her day. Take a swim, do some writing . . .

But the fact that she was allowing Greg to make an appearance in her new life hovered above everything else like a dark cloud.

She was debating whether to even bother to put out snacks to go with the wine he'd promised to bring, not sure just how hospitable to appear, when her cell phone rang. She grabbed it out of her pocketbook, which was sitting on the island. A number, rather than a name, had popped up on the caller ID screen.

"Hello?" she answered, puzzled.

"Good morning, Megan," a male voice greeted her cheerfully.

It took her a second or two to realize it was John.

"Hey, John!" she said. "How's Minneapolis?"

"Cold," he replied. "I just got here and I already miss California. How's the weather there?"

"Beautiful." She glanced out the kitchen window to check.

"How's everything working out so far?"

"Great," she said, grabbing a sponge and idly running it over the countertop. "It took me forever to figure out how the coffeepot works, but that's just because I'm mechanically challenged."

"What about the pool?" he asked. "Have you had a chance to use it yet?"

"Yes," she said, smiling. "I can't tell you how great it felt to be swimming again. Afterwards, I sat next to it, admiring it while I did some writing."

"Good. I'm glad you'll be able to get some use out of it."

"So how's it going out there?"

"Fine. My company is taking good care of me." He hesitated, then asked, "So everything's all right?"

"Everything's fine."

"No floods or fires you're afraid to tell me about?" he asked teasingly.

"Goodness, no!" she cried. "Nothing like that."

"And Endora? Does she miss me?"

"She misses you terribly," Megan said. "She constantly talks about how wonderful you are."

She realized immediately that she'd come off sounding flirtatious. Clearly the conversation with her girlfriends last night had had an effect on her.

In the bright morning light, however, she recognized how ridiculous they had been about even suggesting that John could be a replacement for Greg. Not only was he a complete stranger; he was halfway across the country. Besides, her characterization of him as nerdy was right on.

So she made a point of sounding much more business-like as she added, "But I'm doing my best to make her feel loved." She glanced at the cat, who had yet to look up from her food bowl.

"Good. Give her a hug for me. Or at least an extra cat treat."

"I will. But really, everything is going just fine."

"I'm glad to hear it." After a brief silence, John said, "Well, I just figured I'd check in to make sure there's nothing I forgot to tell you."

"Nope," she replied. "So far, so good."

"I guess you already know your way around Pasadena, so there's no need for me to bore you with a lecture on the best Mediterranean restaurant and my favorite dry-cleaner."

She was beginning to think he'd never get off the phone. But he cleared his throat and said, "Well, don't hesitate to call if anything does come up."

After cleaning up her breakfast dishes, Megan headed to her bedroom, pulling off her shirt and bra en route. As she wriggled into a turquoise two-piece bathing suit, she contemplated what to wear for tonight's reunion with Greg.

Nothing that's too cute or flirty, she decided, like the pink silk dress she'd worn to dinner last night. More like jeans and a T-shirt, to make sure he didn't read too much into her agreeing to see him again.

However, once she was standing at the edge of the diving board, Greg's visit seemed insignificant. The clear blue water beckoned, and for the moment, at least, nothing else seemed to matter.

She stepped onto the diving board and dove in, relishing the sensation of cutting through the water, plunging deeper and deeper below the surface. As she pushed her way back upward, she found herself remembering the fears that once consumed her, tightening her stomach and clouding her mind.

Once again, thinking about Ellie. Hungrily sucking in the air when she resurfaced, appreciating the simple act of breathing, the fact of simply being *alive*.

There really is something terrifying about the water, she thought. And it's not only because of its ability to devour and destroy whoever or whatever dares to take it on. It's also because of the indifference with which it wields its power.

Determined to shake off the painful memories, she began to do laps. She focused on the feeling of gliding through the water, the ease with which she overcame its resistance. After a few seconds, she was able to tune into the strength of her muscles and the comfortable rhythm that propelled her.

Satisfaction surged through her over her ability to maintain control against such a formidable foe and the confidence that came from knowing she'd mastered not only her fears, but the water itself.

Normally a long swim left Megan feeling mellow. Not today.

Once she was out of the water and back in the house, Greg's impending visit loomed ahead once again. She was surprised by how apprehensive she was, how worried she was about what to say and how to act.

She tried to banish her anxiety by writing about it. She spent the rest of the morning sitting by the pool, her hair drying in the sun as she tapped the keys of her laptop. She hoped that putting her feelings into words would make them as insignificant as she wanted them to be.

But her nervousness lingered into the evening. She didn't eat dinner, finding that her stomach was too knotted to accept food. Instead, she perched on a stool in the kitchen, watching Endora gulp down hers. She finally forced herself to pick at the snacks she'd bought for the occasion, the crackers and the pretzels she'd dumped into matching bowls, so she would have at least something in her stomach.

Then she took a long shower, washing her hair and using her favorite honeysuckle-scented body gel. It was manufactured in France, ridiculously expensive and so hard to find that she had to order it online. She dried her hair, shaved her legs, massaged lotion onto her arms and her smooth calves. Despite her discomfort over seeing Greg again, she was determined to look as good as she possibly could.

The next step was putting on her makeup. But as she opened the medicine cabinet door and started grabbing things—blush, eyeliner, mascara—she realized that something was missing.

My lipstick, she thought, frowning. I just bought it last week. Where the heck is it?

She bent over and checked the floor. Not there. She felt around the counter to see if it had slipped behind. But the tile ran right up to the wall.

She wondered if she'd tossed it into her purse before heading out to the Mexican restaurant the night before. But she didn't remember doing that.

Frankly, there's a lot about last night you don't remember, she reminded herself. That's what happens when you drink too many margaritas. Not to mention a chaser of cheap wine.

She decided it would turn up, sooner or later. Besides, a missing lipstick wasn't exactly something to lose sleep over.

Yet the fact that she'd misplaced something, even an item as unimportant as a lipstick, increased her agitation as she stood in front of the closet. She spent a bit more time agonizing over what to wear, finally deciding on a compromise between dressed-up and dressed-down. She grabbed a flowing rayon shirt that had always made her feel good, the fabric a profusion of flowers in pretty shades of blue and green. Then she slipped into jeans.

She waited on the living room couch with Endora in her lap, stroking the cat's thick, silky fur and watching the clock above the fireplace. When the doorbell rang, Megan and Endora both started at the sound.

She placed the cat gently on the carpet, then walked slowly to the front door, taking a deep breath.

It's just for an hour or so, she told herself. You can do this.

"Hi," she said as she opened the door, trying to sound casual. Endora stood behind her, peeking out and staring at this interloper as if she was trying to decide what to make of him.

"Hi, yourself," Greg replied, grinning.

Megan studied him, for some reason surprised by the fact that he looked the same as always. That grin of his, for one thing. She used to think of it as boyish—especially charming because he was two years younger than she was. Tonight, however, it struck her as calculated. Practiced, even, something he'd worked on in order to win people over.

Unlike Megan, Greg was born and raised in southern California, and like his birthplace, he appeared to be all about sunshine and easy living. Even his blond-streaked hair, worn just long enough to allow its natural curliness to flourish, looked as if it was kissed by the sun. He was tall and lean, his shoulders wide and his sun-browned limbs covered with fine, white-blond hair.

But it was his eyes she couldn't keep from staring at. Not only because of their color—an unusually light shade of blue—but even more because they reflected the light in such a way as to look like they were giving off a light of their own.

She noticed that in one hand he was holding a bottle and in the other, a bouquet of flowers.

"For me?" she asked, even though she knew the answer.

"For old times' sake," he said, his smile growing even broader.

Reluctantly she reached for the flowers. "Yellow roses," she said, her voice flat. "Honestly, Greg, you shouldn't have."

"Hey, why not?" he replied. "I know they're your favorite."

She glanced at them, noting that some of the blossoms atop the short stems were edged with brown. Others simply looked a bit withered. She wondered if he'd grabbed them out of the clearance bin.

Typical.

"And what's that?" she asked with the same wariness. "Champagne?"

"Yeah, but I'm afraid it's the cheap stuff." He handed her the bottle. "I know you like that French kind—what's it called? I can never remember the name."

"Moet et Chandon."

"Right. I wanted to get you some of that, but it was out of my price range."

"I'm sure this is fine." Begrudgingly, she muttered, "Thanks."

An awkward moment passed before she stepped aside and said, "So . . . come on in. This, by the way, is Endora. There's no question of who's really in charge here."

But Endora had already returned to the living room couch, leaping up onto the cushions with her usual grace but keeping her eyes on Greg. Megan got the feeling her feline housemate didn't like their visitor, then told herself she was reading way too much into the cat's behavior.

Greg barely glanced at the cat as he strode into the house, his eyes traveling around the living room. "Wow," he said admiringly. "This is some place! You're really staying here for free?"

"That's right. The owner needed somebody to take care of his cat while he's out of town on a business trip."

"That's it?" he asked. "You feed some guy's cat a couple of times a day and you get to live in his house for nothing?"

Megan shrugged. "That's how housesitting works."

"Geez."

"I'm supposed to look after the place, too," she added. "Make sure there aren't any pipes bursting or electrical fires or anything else that would be a disaster if nobody was around."

"Sweet," he said, looking around once again.

"You haven't even seen the pool yet," she said. "It's heated by solar power. I've been using it every day."

"Nice."

"The whole place is gorgeous," she went on, deciding there was no reason to resist the urge to boast. "The kitchen is huge, and I have my own bathroom off the master bedroom. It has a Jacuzzi and an amazing glass shower."

"How long do you have it for?" Greg asked.

"I'm not sure," Megan said. "That's the only downside." Quickly, she added, "But I get the feeling I'm going to be here for a while."

She was aware that she sounded like a proud parent as she added, "John, the man who owns the place, is pretty important. He works for some high-tech company. But they apparently trust him with all kinds of important information. He works at home. In fact, he has a whole roomful of computers and files that are so valuable he has to keep everything locked up."

"The dude obviously makes a ton of money," Greg observed, still taking in his surroundings. "So let's see this pool."

Megan hesitated, wondering if she should lead him into the backyard through her bedroom. Approaching it through the kitchen door was so much less impressive, and it suddenly seemed important for him to see how well she was doing without him.

Even so, she decided to go the kitchen route. As she passed through the kitchen with Greg in tow, she put the flowers and the champagne on the counter. She flicked on the outdoor lights, then stepped onto the patio.

She hadn't paid much attention to how the backyard looked at night, but now, seeing it through Greg's eyes, she realized that it was even more dramatic with the lights glinting off the water's pale turquoise surface.

"Awesome," Greg declared. "You sure lucked out."

He turned to survey the back of the house.

"What room is that?" he asked, pointing at the French doors.

"That's the master bedroom," she said uneasily. "Where I'm staying."

He just nodded. They were silent for a few seconds, until he burst out with, "Hey, how about opening that champagne?"

"Sounds good," she replied, relieved to have a distraction.

Back in the kitchen, Megan picked up the bottle and thrust it at him. "Your job. Opening champagne is something I consider men's work."

With a sly smile, he took it from her. She watched as he wrestled with the cork, unsettled by feeling transported back in time. For a moment, it was as if nothing had changed: the two of them alone together, comfortable in each other's presence, doing a simple, everyday thing.

The loud pop startled them both, even though they were waiting for it.

"Oops, forgot the glasses!" she cried as the bubbling liquid spilled down the sides of the bottle.

Frantically she began opening cabinets. She didn't spot any champagne flutes, so instead she grabbed two of the crystal wine glasses. She held them out while Greg filled them halfway.

"What should we toast?" he asked eagerly, holding up his glass.

"How about . . . to Pasadena real estate?" she suggested.

His disappointment was reflected in his voice as he seconded, "To real estate."

She took a sip, immediately noticing how bad this stuff tasted compared to Moet. Greg had already gulped down most of his, as if the taste barely mattered.

Her eyes lit on the flowers, still lying on the counter.

"I'd better put those in water," she said, jumping up. "I think I saw a vase in the living room."

She retrieved the vase she'd noticed among all the other knickknacks cluttering up the room, then went back into the kitchen and filled it with water. As she stuck in the flowers, she couldn't help noticing how silly they looked in the tall glass vase, with their short stems suspended only halfway down. But she placed them in the middle of the island.

"They're very pretty," she told him, even though she was still focused on their flaws. "Thanks again."

Greg shrugged. "Sure."

She joined him at the island, taking the stool opposite him, rather than next to him.

"So," she said politely, taking another small sip of champagne, "what have you been up to?"

"A lot of things," he replied. "I've been working at a film production company out in Sherman Oaks. They're really doing some great documentaries I'm sworn to secrecy about. Think *Fahrenheit 9/11* and *Waiting for Superman*, but with a Werner Herzog feeling. Really powerful, important stuff. But the job isn't giving me a chance to develop my full creative potential, so I've been thinking seriously about branching into another area. Something more entrepreneurial . . ."

As she sat in silence, letting him talk, she found herself listening to him in a new way. Objectively, like someone who didn't know him very well. His conversation was littered with asides, tangential references to a classic Hitchcock film and a current art exhibition at the Museum of Contemporary Art and a revolutionary discovery that was just written up in *Science*.

This is how he charmed me, she thought, how he kept me enthralled for so long. Greg comes across as someone who knows about everything. But in reality, he knows a little about a lot of things but not a whole lot about any one thing. His skill at sounding impressive, without having anything much to back it up, suddenly seemed to sum him up perfectly.

She started growing bored, waiting for him to shift the focus of the conversation and say, "So tell me, what have you been up to?"

But that didn't happen. Instead, the conversation continued to center around him. A few times, she tried to interject something about her life—the fact that thanks to her housesitting gig she'd been able to get back into swimming, how well her writing was going, even if most of it was journaling—but somehow their chatter always veered back to him.

It could just be that he's nervous about the two of us seeing each other again, she thought. Or maybe it was always like this, and I simply didn't notice.

Her eyes drifted over to the clock above the stove.

"It's almost seven," she said. "Don't you have someplace you're supposed to be?"

"Right. The Lakers game."

"Sounds like fun," she commented, more polite than enthusiastic.

"Should be." He drained the remaining champagne from his glass and stood up. "It was really great seeing you again, Megs."

She averted her eyes and shrugged, not sure how to respond. But then he said, "Y'know, I was thinking that maybe we could, I don't know, catch a movie or something next week."

She took a deep breath. "Greg, I don't think so. There's really no—"

"As friends," he insisted. "I thought we'd agreed we'd still be friends."

I have enough friends, she was tempted to say.

Instead, she replied, "Of course we can be friends. It's just that I expect to be pretty busy for the next few weeks. I really have to focus on finding a job."

He nodded. "In that case, we can play it by ear."

She expected him to move toward the door. Instead, he stood in the same spot, his eyes darting around nervously. She waited, feeling the heaviness of something that wasn't being said, a question that wasn't being asked. Or maybe an explanation for why he'd suddenly decided to barge back into her life.

Finally, she said, "Well, have fun at the game."

"Right," he said, a startled look crossing his face. "The game."

She walked him into the living room, and they stood by the front door. The same awkwardness hovered between them.

"Thanks again for the flowers," she said. "And the champagne."

"Glad you liked it, even though it wasn't that fancy Moet and Chandon stuff you're so crazy about."

She took a step backward in case he was entertaining the idea of kissing her. Instead, he raised his hand and said, "See you."

She watched him head down the driveway, expecting to feel relieved that he was gone. Instead, the sense that something else was going on here tonight, something she doesn't understand, gnawed at her.

That, and the feeling that she hadn't seen the last of him.

CHAPTER 11

H
e stands across the street, among the trees. Watching. Even more prepared this time, since he doesn't know what to expect. He's stuffed a canvas bag with all the things he needs to be comfortable during his vigil: a bottle of water, a couple of granola bars, a flashlight, even a plastic container with a screw-top in case he needs to urinate.

While the sun is low, there's just enough light that he still has a good view of the house.

For the past several hours, there's been no activity. She hasn't left, not even to run errands.

Suddenly his heartbeat quickens.

A car, coming slowly down the street, passes him and continues on to the cul-de-sac. It stops in front of the house.

All his senses are immediately on alert.

One of her girlfriends, stopping by to visit? Someone dropping off a package—or maybe a jacket she accidentally left behind?

His gaze remains steady. When the door on the driver's side opens, the interior light goes on, revealing that there's only one person inside the car.

He freezes when he sees who gets out.

A guy around thirty, probably, given his build and the way he's dressed. He's carrying something. Two things: a bottle in one hand, a small bouquet of what appear to be yellow roses in the other.

An intruder, he thinks. His heart pounds violently, reverberating through his chest. Maybe he's just a friend, he tells himself. Or someone who has the wrong address.

But the intruder heads up the front walk jauntily, heading toward the door. Cocky. Confident. As if he belongs there. It could still be some sort of mistake . . .

He squints, struggling to see. The light next to the front door is on, even though it's not yet dark, and he sees the intruder raise his arm. He's ringing the bell. Maybe she won't answer. But after only a few seconds, the front door swings open.

A minute passes. He lets out a cry of frustration, desperately wishing he had a better view. And that he could hear them.

Then he sees the intruder step into the house. The front door closes.

A sick feeling comes over him. *This isn't supposed to happen.*

He stands perfectly still in the dark for a few seconds, his thoughts whirling so fast he can barely focus. And then, in a flash, he decides.

I've got to know what's going on in there. I have to go inside.

He hesitates, aware of the risk he's taking. But only a moment passes before he crosses the street, making a point of strolling in a relaxed, normal manner. The last thing he wants to do is call attention to himself.

As he nears the house, he is gripped by anxiety. The palms of his hands are slick as they clench the things he's brought, his stomach is knotted, his heart pounds so loudly he's afraid the whole neighborhood can hear it.

He's thankful that by now it's almost dark. And that the cul-de-sac is as desolate as always.

From the edge of the property, he can see that the living room light is on. But he can't see anyone inside.

He decides they must be in another part of the house. The possibility that they could be in the bedroom flashes through his mind, but he immediately banishes it.

No.

The closer to the house he gets, the more cautious he becomes. It's possible that she'll happen to glance out the window—or that the intruder could come out again to get something from his car. He stays close to the bushes in case he has to duck, glad the yard is filled with such lush vegetation.

So far, so good.

He goes around to the side of the house, to the door leading to the basement. But when he gets near, the sound of voices makes him freeze.

"You sure lucked out."

A male voice, no doubt the cocky guy who arrived at the house bearing flowers. His blood boils at the sound of it. It reflects his cool, easy-going personality, his sense of entitlement, his attitude that everything in life is simply there for the taking.

"What room is that?" the same voice asks.

"That's the master bedroom," he hears her reply. "Where I'm staying."

He stands perfectly still, waiting to hear what she says next. But after a few moments of silence, it's the intruder who speaks.

"Hey, how about opening that champagne?"

"Sounds good," she says.

He hears footsteps on the patio, a sign that they're heading back inside. Quickly he slips in through the basement door, aware that they're less likely to hear him if they're still on the patio.

He closes the heavy door behind him, then climbs down the concrete steps, grasping the wooden handrail and using the flashlight's dim beam to guide him.

But almost immediately he discovers there's something he didn't anticipate: lingering here in this small, dark space, enclosed by windowless gray cinderblock walls, carries him back to The Lost Place.

Before he has a chance to convince himself that that's all behind him, nothing more than a nightmarish memory, he feels the room closing in on him. He's cast back in time to when he was twelve years old. He feels the same way he felt then. Frightened. Alone. Completely out of control.

He sinks down to the concrete floor, hard against his knees. He covers his face with his hands and lets out a whimpering sound. But it's not enough to keep him from retreating.

He can see it all, replaying in his head with such clarity that it becomes real.

It's early in the morning, 6:30. Cold and gray outside. Cold and gray inside, too.

If there's any heat in the building, he can't feel it. As for the grayness, it's the color of the walls, the floors, the bars on the windows, the guards' uniforms.

They're supposed to refer to them as counselors. But they're really guards.

He's in a bathroom, the gray tile floor icy beneath his bare feet. He stands with nine other boys in front of a long line of sinks. He turns on the faucet, but even the water from the warm tap runs cool. He tries not to shiver, since the other boys might think he's afraid.

It's important never to appear afraid.

There's no talking allowed, and while the other boys complain about this policy, he finds it a relief. He doesn't want to talk to them. He doesn't want to talk to anyone.

Some of the boys are mentally ill. They talk to themselves, they scream for no reason, they scratch at their faces, trying to get rid of bugs that aren't really there. Many of the boys take medication, which makes them listless and dull.

He sometimes wishes that he, too, were crazy. Or that he could take the pills that make it so hard for the boys who take them to keep their eyes open. Then, maybe The Lost Place wouldn't bother him so much.

But he has no such relief. Every minute he's locked up in there seems unduly long. It's as if time has been forgotten, just like the boys themselves.

He knows he doesn't belong there.

They never should have put me in here, he tells himself over and over. I didn't do anything wrong. It's not like I ever intended to hurt Caroline.

And then, abruptly, he's drawn back to the present by the sound of voices coming from upstairs, in the kitchen.

He can hear her.

Megan.

Simply hearing her speak is enough to bring him back to the present. He rises to his feet, exhausted but filled with relief.

A few seconds later, he's able to focus on what she's saying.

"What should we toast?" the intruder asks.

"To Pasadena real estate," she replies.

"To real estate," he repeats, his voice flat.

He lowers himself onto the bottom step, clasping the water bottle in his hand. He hears her moving around upstairs, running the water in the kitchen sink, telling the intruder how pretty the flowers are.

He sits without moving a muscle—something he's very good at—and listens. Their conversation is dull, mostly about *him.* The job he's working at, the movies he's seeing, the books he's reading, blah, blah, blah . . .

Stupid jerk, he thinks.

But he listens carefully, trying to figure out their relationship.

"It's almost seven," he finally hears her say. "Don't you have someplace you're supposed to be?"

More chitchat, then: "I was thinking that maybe we could catch a movie or something next week."

"Greg, I don't think so," she replies, sounding annoyed. "There's really no—"

"As friends," the intruder interrupts. "I thought we'd agreed we'd still be friends."

So he's *not* her boyfriend, he thinks, lightheaded with relief. At least not any more. Still, he's glad that they talk just a little while longer and then Megan's visitor leaves.

He's gone, he thinks. *Finally.*

Yet his relief is short-lived. Even after the intruder is gone, a bad feeling eats away at him.

The fact that another guy has come to the house, even someone Megan doesn't seem interested in, is a wake-up call. A reminder that there are plenty of guys out there who'd do anything to have her all to themselves. Men who'd go to any length, who'd do whatever it takes, to make her belong to them.

Just like him.

CHAPTER 12

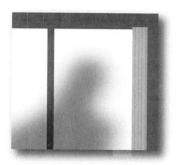

Saturday morning, Megan woke up to find that her head was clouded. Not from margaritas this time, not from champagne, but from an unsettled feeling that she'd opened a door she should have keep closed.

What were you thinking? she berated herself. Why on *earth* did you let Greg come over?

It wasn't until Endora leaped onto the bed, loudly demanding breakfast, that she dragged herself out of bed. Pulling a sweater over her sleep shirt, she padded barefoot into the kitchen with the fluffy orange cat trotting beside her, pulling her hair up into a messy knot she fastened with an elastic band.

Coffee, she told herself. That's all you need.

She sat at the island, gulping down a cup as she watched her charge daintily eat her breakfast. But today, even caffeine failed to work its usual magic. The feeling that she'd made a terrible mistake persisted.

She decided to do what she usually did when she was in a bad mood: perform a task that helped her regain control of her life.

Megan poured herself another cup and settled back onto the tall stool, this time with Endora in her lap. She opened her computer on the island.

She forgot all about the coffee cooling beside her as she tapped away at the keys. But rather than answering emails or spewing out random thoughts in her journal, this morning she was jotting down facts. The company names and dates of her summer jobs at college, a recounting of her responsibilities at Hayworth, a list of special skills that a potential employer might find attractive.

She hoped she could turn these facts into a résumé that would stand out from all the others currently being emailed around the country by the unemployed.

She suspected that her sudden burst of energy was the result of Greg resurfacing. Despite her annoyance over him trying to wheedle his way back onto her A list, seeing him again turned out a useful reminder of why she'd crossed him off in the first place—and how very different the two of them were.

Don't let this happen to you, she thought with a wry smile.

As she read and reread the succinct yet telling phrases she'd composed— "strong speaking and writing abilities in French and Spanish," "self-starter who enjoys working independently"—she was aware that she wasn't exactly an expert when it came to converting them into a professional-looking document. And that was what she needed, a piece of paper that would capture the attention of Human Resources people and other individuals with the power to bestow employment upon her.

She started when the doorbell chimed.

Greg?

It was the first thought that popped into her head. She immediately tried to banish it, instead seeking a more logical explanation.

It's probably somebody looking for John, she thought, reminding herself that he was the one who really lived here. The UPS man, someone from the power company, a volunteer collecting money for some cause.

She was startled to find a teenage boy waiting on the other side of the door, his face studded with acne.

"Delivery," he announced. He held out an elongated white box, as if to prove his point.

Megan looked past him and saw a white PT Cruiser on the driveway, behind her car. The words "Jacob Maarse Florists" and "Special Delivery" were stenciled on the side.

"Flowers?" she asked uncertainly, wondering if perhaps he'd gotten the wrong house.

"That's what we do," the boy replied cheerfully. "This is 55 Sierra Avenue, right?"

Reluctantly she took the box from him. Even though it was now in her hands, he continued to stand there, his expression expectant.

"Oh," Megan exclaimed, finally understanding. "Hold on. Let me get my pocketbook." She rushed back inside and grabbed her wallet.

"Here you go," she said, presenting a ten-dollar bill to the delivery boy.

"Hey, thanks!" he exclaimed, his face lighting up.

"No problem," she returned, chagrined over having clearly over-tipped.

As she watched the delivery car back out of the driveway, she noticed someone standing near the curb.

Russell. Again. The irritating kid from down the street. This time without his furry sidekick. Having no choice but to acknowledge him, she gave a half-hearted wave. "Hey, Russell."

"Hi, Megan!" he called energetically. "All settled in?"

"Pretty much," she replied. "Thanks for asking."

He took a few steps closer, but she pointedly closed the door. But not before seeing the expression on his face, a mixture of surprise and anger.

She'd already forgotten all about him as she went back into the kitchen, eyeing the long white box on the counter as if it contained a bomb.

"I can't believe Greg sent me flowers," she muttered to Endora.

The orange Maine coon, stretched out in a patch of sun by the back door, barely looked up.

Megan's hands were shaking as she opened the box. Yet once she did, she couldn't help gasping. Inside were a dozen yellow roses, just like the night before. But that was where the resemblance ended, since these were elegant, long-stemmed blossoms that immediately filled the entire kitchen with the sweet fragrance she loved so much.

"These are gorgeous," she half-whispered as she took them out of the box, the crisp green tissue paper rustling. "In fact, these are the most beautiful roses I've ever seen."

She glanced over at the scraggly bouquet Greg had brought over the night before, still sitting on the island. They looked pathetic compared to these, their stems comically short and their pale yellow petals drooping sadly.

She pulled last night's roses out of their crystal vase and stuck them into a drinking glass she half-filled with water. Not knowing what else to do with them, she pushed them toward the back of the counter, out of the way.

Next she gently placed the vase in the sink and pawed through the tissue paper, searching for the packet of flower food. She found it, along with a small white envelope.

Filled with dread, she slit it open and pulled out the small white rectangle inside.

"*Thanks for being in my life*," it read.

Just seeing the words made her stomach sink.

Now you've done it, she scolded herself. Letting Greg come over was even a bigger mistake than you thought.

But she couldn't deny that these flowers deserved royal treatment. She dumped the packet of powder into the vase, then filled it with water. She carefully put in one rose at a time after plucking off the water-filled plastic vials at the end of each stem, doing her best to arrange the luxuriant bouquet attractively. She'd just finished when her cell phone rang.

Greg, she thought with dread, considering not answering even as she grabbed her phone out of her pocketbook. When she glanced at caller ID, she was pleased to see that it wasn't Greg after all.

"Hey, Megan, it's John," the voice at the other end greeted her.

"Hey, John," she replied, her tone reflecting her relief.

"I hope I'm not calling too early," he said.

"No, not at all," she assured him politely. "I've been up for a while."

"Great. I just called to see if you got the flowers."

"Flowers?" she repeated.

They're from *John?* She felt as if a great weight had been lifted off her shoulders as she glanced over at the bouquet, the twelve perfect yellow blossoms rising gracefully out of the kitchen sink. In her eyes, they had already started looking even more beautiful.

"You mean they haven't come yet—and I spoiled the surprise?"

The sound of John's voice at the other end of the line jolted her back to the moment.

"No, they were just delivered a few minutes ago," she said. Enthusiastically, she added, "Thank you so much. They're absolutely amazing!"

"You're welcome." He hesitated before adding, "I hoped you'd get the symbolism."

"Symbolism?" Megan repeated, her forehead furrowing.

"Pasadena, the City of Roses? I made a little joke about that when we met at Peet's the first time, but maybe you missed it."

"Of course I remember," Megan replied, feeling silly for not making the connection.

"At first, I was going to get red, but I decided that was kind of a cliché," John went on. "So I went with yellow instead. I hope you like them."

"I *love* them," she gushed. "In fact, yellow roses are my absolute favorite."

"No kidding!" He laughed again. "Gee, I guess I really lucked out on that one. Actually, the woman who answered the phone at the florist recommended going with the yellow, so I can't take full credit."

It was only then that she remembered the message on the card.

Thanks for being in my life.

"I was a little . . . surprised by the message on the card," she commented.

"Oh, gee," John replied, sighing. "I hope I didn't go overboard. I just wanted to say thanks for all you're doing for me. I don't know what I would have done if you hadn't come along.

"You see, I was frantic about finding somebody responsible, somebody I could trust, to take care of my house," he continued. "And Endora, of course. Naturally, she's my main concern. And all this happened so fast, finding out I was being sent out of town and all . . . Well, I just wanted you to know how much I value you. And everything you're doing for me."

"It's working out well for me, too," she told him sincerely.

"I'm so glad." After a short silence, he said, "Well, I guess I'd better get back to work."

"On a Saturday?" she asked, startled.

"I'm afraid so," he replied. With a deep sigh, he added, "I'm in the middle of a huge project, and everything that could possibly go wrong has already gone wrong. I'm going to be dealing with this twenty-four/seven until I figure out how to fix it."

"Sounds like a total nightmare," she said sympathetically. "I'll let you go, then."

After they'd said good-bye, Megan remained standing in the middle of the kitchen, staring at the bouquet.

They're so pretty, she thought. Especially now that I know they're from John—and not Greg. Still, as she placed the display in the middle of the kitchen island, an uncomfortable feeling nagged at her.

I suppose John has gobs of money, she thought, but sending an extravagant gift like this seems so . . . unnecessary.

Then there was the message on the card. She wondered if he was trying to tell her something more than that he was happy she was housesitting for him—like that he was interested in her in another way.

Or maybe he's just one of those people who's not good with words, she mused, wanting to consider every possible angle. In fact, maybe he told the florist over the phone that he didn't know what to write, and the woman who took his order actually wrote it for him. I bet she's somebody who's read too many romance novels, and so she went a little overboard.

The giddiness of relief quickly returned, making her eager to jump into a new day. She was about to head to the shower when her cell phone rang again. Checking caller ID, she saw that this time it was a friend from Hayworth she hadn't talked to since she'd left the company.

"Hey, Megan!" Rachel greeted her. "Any chance you're free tonight? A bunch of us were talking about going to this hot new club in Westwood, and I found myself thinking that I haven't seen you in ages. Want to come along?"

Go out and have fun, Megan told herself, as if a well-meaning friend or parent were residing inside her head. You deserve it, especially given how well things are going.

So even before she heard the details, she knew she'd say yes.

CHAPTER 13

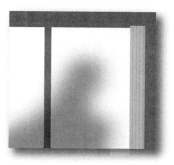

Megan spent her Saturday luxuriating in another perfect day of writing, swimming, and relishing her solitude. Endora was truly the perfect housemate: eager to cuddle whenever she craved companionship, yet making it clear she needed plenty of alone time herself.

Still, by the time she threw together a quick dinner of soup, a carton of yogurt, and a handful of cookies, Megan was ready to spend the evening out. After long hours of silence, she welcomed a night in a room packed with people and vibrating with music so loud she would barely be able to hear her own thoughts.

She took her time getting dressed, choosing a short red dress and her black heels. She put on her makeup with a slightly heavier hand than usual, bemoaning the fact that she'd forgotten to replace her missing lipstick. Instead, she ended up wearing a bright red lipstick she found at the bottom of her purse, a shade she'd always thought was too intense but couldn't bring herself to throw away.

Even though this was only her third day at John's house, she'd already developed what she thought of as her usual routine before going out for the evening: She filled Endora's food and water bowls, made sure all the lights and appliances were turned off, and checked the back door to make sure it was shut tight.

Even though she was eager to get the evening underway, she remembered to turn on a light in the living room, since the porch light illuminated little beyond the front door. It was dusk as she left the house, ruminating about the best way to cross practically the entire city. Saturday night traffic on the freeways was bound to be as bad as it was during rush hour, and she was completely absorbed in trying to construct the best route.

The last thing she expected was that someone was watching her. But as she neared her car, she noticed someone in the street, standing in the shadows. Even though there was no yappy dog with him, she immediately knew who it was.

She quickened her pace, looking straight ahead and pretending she hadn't noticed him. She'd just made it to her car when he called, "Hey, Megan!"

She glanced up, doing her best to look surprised, as if she'd just realized he was there. "Oh, hello, Russell," she said evenly, trying not to sound too friendly. By that point, Megan had unlocked her car and was poised to slide into the front seat.

"So . . . are you going out tonight?" Russell asked, walking toward her. As he grew closer, she saw that he was doing his peculiar blinking thing.

"That's right. I'm going to a club in Westwood."

"Sounds fun," he said, his voice hollow.

The awkward silence that followed caused a wave of sympathy to sweep over her. "What about you?" she asked. "Got any plans for tonight?"

"No," he answered. And then: "I mean, nothing definite, at least not yet. I'll probably hang out with some of my friends. That's what I usually do on Saturday nights. In fact, they're probably trying to call me right now. Stupid me, I left my cell phone at home."

"Well, have a nice time!" she said. She waved, more anxious than ever to be on her way.

"Right," Russell replied. "See you, Megan!"

What a creepy kid, she thought as she headed down Sierra Avenue.

Checking the rear view mirror, she noticed that, as usual, he was standing near the driveway, his eyes fixed on her car.

Suddenly she softened, for the first time feeling sorry for him. He can't help it that he's so geeky, she reminded herself.

She hoped he'd been telling the truth when he said he'd be hanging out with friends tonight. She hated to think of such a pathetic soul all alone on a Saturday night, with nothing to do.

What that boy really needs, she thought, is a girlfriend.

But she was looking forward to her own night out too much to dwell on the problems of someone she hardly knew. She forgot all about Russell and the questionable state of his social life as she veered onto the Foothill Freeway and started making her way toward L.A.

Of course she's going out tonight, he thinks grimly, watching the red taillights of Megan's car come on.

It's Saturday night, the first one she's spent in the house. Saturday is the night that people go out. Drinking, dancing, partying, who knows what else.

Still, he tells himself that she's not like the rest of them. For one thing, she doesn't have a new boyfriend to replace that loser who came over the night before.

At least not yet.

Even so, he's dismayed by how she looked as she got into her car. Wearing a dress that's much too short and those shoes of hers that are much too high.

Makeup, too. Plenty of it. Much too much of it.

His breathing becomes labored, and his heart pounds with jackhammer speed.

She's probably getting together with some girlfriends, he tells himself, taking deep breaths. That's what girls do when they don't have a guy to spend their Saturday night with, isn't it?

He's convinced himself that that's exactly what she has planned as her car begins backing slowly out of the driveway. But the fact that she's leaving makes his heartbeat quicken even more.

Should I follow her?

There's something appealing about the idea of getting in the car and driving after her. Watching her while she's out in the world. Moving to the music on a dance floor, laughing, having fun.

But there are a hundred reasons not to get in the car and follow her. She might spot him in her rear-view mirror. He could lose sight of her car in traffic and get lost. He could trail her to a different part of the city, only to see her disappear behind the doors of some trendy club that would never in a million years let him in.

Even more, he realizes, he doesn't *want* to have an image of her giggling with her friends, bumping into strangers, making small talk with whatever man decides to sidle over to her as she stands at a bar. After all, she belongs to him now.

The same way Caroline did. At least for a little while.

He's already decided on his plans by the time he watches the red taillights grow smaller and smaller, finally disappearing at the end of Sierra Avenue.

Tonight, I'll stay in.

He continues to stand in the same spot, concerned that she might come back for some forgotten item.

Five minutes. Ten minutes.

Patience is something he's mastered. But finally, he can't wait any longer. He walks toward the house, as usual acting as if there's absolutely nothing out of the ordinary going on. As he crosses the front yard, he pretends to look straight ahead but moves his eyes from side to side, making sure no one else is around.

No one who can see what he's doing.

But there's not a soul in sight. Not even any lights on in the house next door, separated from this house by a veritable forest.

The porch light is on, and she's left a lamp on in the living room once again. She's clearly someone who doesn't like coming home to a dark house. It's a good policy for a single young woman who's living on her own, he thinks approvingly. It never hurts to take every safety precaution possible.

He walks around to the side of the house, slipping inside through the basement. Even though he doesn't linger, just being in that small space makes him shudder.

He hurries up the stairs, to the main floor. When he steps into the hallway, he sees there are no lights on in the rest of the house.

He's still debating whether or not he dares turn one on when he jumps at the feeling of something brushing against his leg. He looks down and sees it's only the cat.

"You again," he says, his tone gruff.

The animal meows, looking up at him imploringly.

But he forgets all about the cat as he heads toward the bedroom. *Her* bedroom.

It's dark inside, the illumination from the living room not reaching this far back. He hesitates in the doorway, once again wondering if he should flick on the lights. But he's already certain no one is watching. Not on this isolated cul-de-sac. He boldly flips on the light switch.

He sits on the edge of her bed, looking around the room at her possessions, resting his palms against the smooth fabric of the bedspread. This is the place where she gets dressed, where she plans her day, where she sleeps and dreams. For him, it's enough just to be in here.

For now.

He reaches over and runs his fingertips along her pillow. *This is the place where she rests her head every night.* Then he moves his hand along the bed, picturing the outline of her body.

This is where her shoulders are, this is where her hips are . . .

He shivers, finding the ecstasy almost too much to bear. He looks around the room, his heartbeat quickening when he spots a flash of red on the closet floor, mixed in with a jumble of other clothes. He immediately recognizes it: the shirt she wore the day before yesterday, the day she moved in.

He grabs it, then stretches out on the far side of the bed, lying next to the spot where he imagines she sleeps. He unzips his pants and with one hand shoves the red shirt inside. Then he closes his eyes, blocking out the rest of the world so he can see only her. He thinks about how she looked on moving day, her skin glistening with perspiration, strands of her shiny dark brown hair cascading around her face, the curves of her taut body clearly visible through her tight red shirt and her shorts . . .

He imagines her leaning over him, here in this bed, wanting him as much as he wants her. Not only desiring him, but also seeing him for who he really is, accepting him, even loving him.

He's close to climaxing, just seconds away, when he suddenly feels something hitting his chest. His eyes fly open, and he finds himself looking into a feline face.

"*Damn you!*" he yells, jolting upright so suddenly that the cat flies off the bed. His desire is already gone, completely dissipated by feelings of surprise and anger. "Get the hell *out* of here!"

The cat turns to glower at him, meowing angrily, then skitters off.

He jumps off the bed, still furious.

"Damn!" he sputters. "Stupid animal!"

Angrily he tosses the shirt back onto the closet floor. He stands in the middle of the room, his breath coming fast and heavy and his mind racing. He spots the cat again, this time standing in the doorway. Glaring at him, its eyes glowing menacingly.

He lunges for the animal, digging his fingers into its flesh so tightly that it yowls. But his grip is strong, and he holds it away from him so that it can't scratch or bite.

He steps out into the hallway, opens the door directly opposite the bedroom, and tosses the cat into the linen closet, slamming the door before it can escape. Through the door, he can hear its angry meows, but he has no trouble blocking out the noise.

He goes back into Megan's bedroom. Glances around, desperately looking for something to calm him down. His eyes light on the dresser, where her things are scattered across the top.

He walks over and begins picking them up, one at a time. A hairbrush. Sunglasses. A pair of earrings, simple gold hoops. He can feel his agitation drain away as he cradles each item lovingly, stroking it, sniffing it, holding it against his heart.

Trying to absorb her. To make Megan even more a part of him.

He begins opening drawers. Touching her things at first, but opening other drawers, too. First a drawer of neatly folded sweaters, then the one below. He runs his hands distractedly across a stack of shirts, frowning when he notices that the green one on the bottom juts out at an odd angle, not aligned with all the rest.

When he walks into the hallway, he tunes in to the cat's howls but just as quickly tunes them out again. He steps into the kitchen and turns on the overhead light. He's delighted to see signs of her everywhere in here, too. She's rinsed out a plate and a drinking glass and left them on the drainboard to dry. Her collection of groceries is still neatly lined up on the counter, and her laptop sits on the island.

She's so much at home here, he thinks, overflowing with happiness. As if she expects to stay a long, long time.

He's about to leave the house when a shock of color catches his eye.

A bouquet of yellow roses. From *him*. Even though she acted as if she doesn't care about him, she's got them on display.

As if they matter to her. As if she *cherishes* them. As if what she says and how she acts don't tell the whole truth.

Jealousy explodes inside him with the uncontrollable force of a tidal wave. It sweeps over him, blocking out all reason, clouding his brain.

He can focus on only one thing. *Retaliation.*

His hands tremble as he zigzags around the kitchen, yanking open cabinets and drawers, angrily slamming them shut. Finally, he spots what he's been looking for. A hammer, nestled in a drawer with other household tools.

He reaches down and closes his fingers around the wooden handle. Just holding it in his hand calms him, as if simply knowing he's about to act is enough to diminish his feelings of powerlessness.

CHAPTER 14

Driving along Sierra Avenue at two a.m., Megan was struck by how eerie the neighborhood seemed at night. The houses she passed were just as grand as always, the landscaping just as luxurious. But with not a single light shining from any of the windows, and not a soul in sight, she realized how desolate this area was. No restaurants, no gas stations, not even a 7-Eleven.

She was glad she had her wits about her. She'd learned her lesson at Acapulco the other evening and taken things easier tonight, switching to club soda after only two drinks.

She reached the cul-de-sac, which was even more secluded. Tonight, it struck her as darker than usual.

As soon as she pulled into the driveway, she understood why. While the living room light was on, just as she'd left it, the light on the front porch was out.

Great, she thought with chagrin. It figures that I don't remember seeing any spare bulbs anywhere in the house. Of course, I can always go out and buy some.

But the practicalities of a new household chore weren't what concerned her. The darkness, the silence that surrounded her, now seemed forbidding. Dangerous even.

As she got out of her car, she reminded herself that there was probably no place in the entire world that was safer than Pasadena. Yet she couldn't help feeling uneasy. She already had her house key in her hand as she walked up the driveway, looking from side to side and listening for anything out of the ordinary.

When she reached the front door, she felt a hard crunch beneath her feet. She glanced down, the lamp in the window providing enough light for her to see the shards of glass scattered across the landing.

Instinctively she looked up. As she feared, the glass was from the porch light. Both the glass panels of the shade and the bulb inside it had been smashed, leaving jagged edges that loomed above her head.

"Oh, my God. What happened?" she cried, even though there was no one around to hear.

Vandalism? she wondered, her heart pounding wildly and her mouth tasting of metal. Or maybe there was an earthquake here in Pasadena while I was on the other side of the city? But during the entire drive home, she'd had her car radio tuned to a local station, one with regular traffic reports. There'd been no mention of an earthquake.

Suddenly all she wanted was to get inside. She let herself in and quickly locked the door behind her. She'd barely gotten in before she froze. She heard something, a noise she hadn't heard here in the house before.

A rustling, something she couldn't identify.

The sound of something—or someone—moving.

It was coming from the back of the house.

Her mouth was dry, her heart pounding so loudly it was hard for her to hear.

"Hello?" she called, taking a step across the living room, toward the back of the house. "Is anyone here?"

Of course there's no one here, she told herself.

Yet she had the disturbing feeling she wasn't alone.

Should I call the police? she wondered, her mind racing. Or get back in the car and drive away?

Part of her felt ridiculous, as if she was overreacting. The broken porch light could have been caused by a falling tree branch. And the rustling sound could have been anything: the wind, a bush brushing against the house, even a rodent in the wall.

The idea of fleeing seemed overly dramatic. As for the police, they'd probably write her off as a crazy woman.

This is my house, Megan reminded herself. At least for now. The main reason I'm living here is that I'm supposed to be taking care of it.

She took a few more steps, determined to ignore her racing heart and investigate the mysterious noise.

And then she heard a muffled *meow*.

"Endora!" she cried aloud, her voice breathless with relief.

Scolding herself for not realizing the source of the noise right from the start, she hurried to the back of the house. Following the cat's woeful cries, she headed for the linen closet and pulled open the door.

"You silly pussycat!" she cried as she scooped Endora into her arms. Nuzzling her face against the cat's soft fur, she demanded, "What have you been up to while I was out?"

Meowing angrily, Endora wriggled out of her grasp and leaped to the floor. It was as if she'd already spent enough time being locked up and had no intention of letting it happen again.

As she watched the cat lope into the kitchen, Megan frowned.

Did I leave the linen closet door ajar? she wondered as the thirsty animal eagerly lapped up water from her bowl.

She rubbed her forehead, trying to remember if she'd even opened that closet since she got here. She remembered John pointing it out to her when he showed her around. But she'd only been here for three days—and during that time she'd had no reason to go looking for sheets or towels.

John must have left it open before he left on Thursday, she decided, and I guess I just never noticed. Endora must have slipped in there while I was out and I guess a breeze slammed it shut.

That's got to be what happened, she told herself, comforted by such a common-sense explanation.

By that point Megan was more than ready for sleep. She retreated to her bedroom, where she wriggled out of her dress and climbed into bed.

Despite her fatigue, an uncomfortable feeling still nagged at her. She lay stiffly, her muscles taut and her temples throbbing.

The strange noise turned out to be nothing, she told herself, trying to reason her agitation away. As for the broken porch light, you'll talk to John about it tomorrow. There's probably some obvious explanation, and once it all makes sense you'll feel silly.

To stop her ruminations, she forced herself to concentrate on something pleasant. By thinking about how lovely it was to have this big, comfortable bed all to herself, she finally managed to drift off.

Morning's bright light streaming through the sheer white curtains dragged Megan into consciousness.

She immediately realized she'd been better off asleep. Even though she hadn't drunk much the night before, her head was pounding, its rhythm echoing the pulsating music at the club. But while that beat had been electrifying, this throbbing simply made her feel as if her head would explode if she moved even the slightest.

That's what you get for staying out so late, she told herself.

The idea of rolling over and going back to sleep seemed irresistible. And then she remembered something else that made the idea of pulling the covers over her head so appealing. She had a new task to deal with: the broken porch light.

But it wasn't the logistics of cleaning up the glass shards and finding a replacement shade that she dreaded. It was telling John about it—which in her mind was the same as admitting that she wasn't doing a perfect job of keeping his house safe and sound.

She'd just yanked the blankets up to her chin when the familiar feeling of tiny feet marching across her thighs reminded her that she had other responsibilities that weren't as easy to put off.

"Go away!" she barked, her voice thick.

Endora meowed loudly, her soft, furry face next to Megan's. She cursed the cat for being so smart—and for insisting on such a rigid schedule when it came to meals.

She'd already learned enough about her feline housemate to know she wasn't about to back down. Besides, she reminded herself, the poor kitty cat had had a traumatic night, spending most of the evening shut up in a linen closet. She deserved to be treated well.

Megan was still trying to force herself out of bed when her cell phone rang.

"Go away," she said again, aware that the sound was coming from all the way across the room.

The melodious ringing persisted. While she was tempted to ignore it, she couldn't do the same with Endora's persistent meowing. She had no choice but to get up.

She hauled herself to a sitting position, squinting in the bright sunlight. She spotted her pocketbook on the floor, lying next to the red dress she'd barely managed to pull off before dropping onto the bed last night.

Or technically, this morning.

The pounding in her head grew stronger as she dragged herself up and kneeled in front of her pocketbook. She rooted around, finally finding her phone.

"Hello?" she answered, doing her best to sound normal. Endora, meanwhile, was meowing so loudly she was certain that whoever was calling could hear her.

"Megan?" The voice was John's. "Is that you?"

"It's me."

"You sound different. I guess I woke you up. Sorry."

"That's okay," she insisted. "I was awake."

Standing up, she caught sight of her reflection in the mirror over the dresser. Mussed up hair, eyes barely more than slits, smeared mascara and eye shadow that made her look like a raccoon . . .

"But it sounds like you're still in bed," John went on, sounding apologetic.

Megan resisted the urge to make an excuse, to explain that she'd been out late last night. She didn't want to sound flighty or irresponsible, especially when she was about to tell him about the porch light. Besides, she didn't want him to think she was neglecting his beloved cat who she'd become so fond of that she'd already started to dread the day she had to leave.

"I love to sleep in on Sunday mornings," she told him. "I'm usually pretty disciplined, but this is one indulgence I can't resist. What time is it, anyway?"

"Eleven o'clock," he said. "At least, in California."

"Definitely time for me to get out of bed," she said. "Besides, I wanted to talk to you today anyway."

"Really?" he said lightly. "Is there a problem?"

"Sort of. When I came back last night, the light on the front porch was broken."

"You mean the bulb burned out? I can tell you where I store the extras."

"The glass panels on the fixture were broken, too." She hesitated. "Shattered, as if something had hit them."

"Huh. That's odd."

John's reaction made her heart sink. So much for hoping he'd come up with a common sense explanation, she thought.

But she immediately felt better when he added, "The wind probably blew something against it. But it wasn't expensive, and it shouldn't be hard tracking down a replacement."

"So it's not that big a deal?" Megan asked, relieved.

"Of course not," he replied. "I'll take care of it when I get back."

"I'm so glad you're not furious with me," she said.

He sounded surprised as he asked, "Why would I be?"

"Because I'm supposed to be taking care of your house."

"Things around a house get broken," he said. "That's what happens when people live there."

Of course everything he was saying made complete sense. But she still felt as if a weight had been lifted from her shoulders. Not only because he wasn't mad, but also because he seemed so matter-of-fact about it, as if a shattered light fixture was an everyday occurrence.

"So," she asked, "is there anything in particular you called about?"

Still clasping the phone next to her ear, Megan shuffled into the kitchen. Endora followed, still meowing but sounding much more optimistic.

"I'm afraid there's something else I'm going to ask you to do for me," he said.

"Anything," she replied distractedly.

She crouched in front of the cabinet and pulled out the bag of cat food. Endora cheered her on as she scooped out the breakfast portion and dropped it into her bowl, the hard kibbles banging loudly against the ceramic.

"Before I left, I made arrangements with a gardening service," he told her. "At least, I thought I did. But I just called them to find out when they'd be coming, and it seems they've gone out of business."

"Okay," she said. "So what do you need me to do?"

Now that Endora was chowing down happily, Megan turned toward the coffee pot. She knew that two cups with a side order of Advil would return her head to normalcy. In fact, she could hardly wait for them to kick in.

But as she headed over to the counter, she suddenly cried out.

Lying on the kitchen floor was the water glass she'd used for Greg's roses, smashed into a hundred tiny pieces. Languishing in the puddle were the flowers themselves, withered and brown and incredibly sad.

"Is everything okay?" John asked anxiously.

"It's nothing," she assured him quickly. "Just a broken glass. Endora must have jumped up onto the counter and knocked it over."

"It's a bad habit," he said, "one I've tried to break her of. She doesn't do it often, though, just when she's angry. I don't suppose you left her alone recently."

"I did," Megan admitted, leaning over and gingerly picking up the larger chunks of glass. "I went out with some friends last night. I guess she didn't like it. Still, it's the first time she's done anything like this."

"Were you out late?" John asked.

"Yes, as a matter of fact."

"That's probably why, then. She gets upset if she's left alone in the house late at night."

While John's explanation made perfect sense, the fact that two different glass items had been broken in the same night struck Megan as odd. Especially since they were located in completely different parts of the house.

I guess it's just a coincidence, she thought.

But somehow, that rationalization didn't make the strangeness go away.

Distractedly, she said, "I'm really sorry about the glass. I'll replace it, if you'd like."

"Don't worry about it," he insisted. "Anyway, about the gardener falling through . . . I was wondering if you'd mind filling in. I'm not talking about anything heavy-duty. I was hoping you'd be willing to do some watering."

"Sure," she said, trying to focus on what he was saying. "I can handle that."

"It's just that it would be difficult to find a replacement from Minnesota," he went on. "Calling a bunch of places and finding out what they'd charge and all that. Besides, they'd probably want to stop by to take a look around before giving me a price. I wouldn't want to tie you up by making you wait for them to come by."

"Of course," she said. "Thanks for being so considerate."

"No problem. So here's what I'd like you to do," John said. "There's a sprinkler in front, so that's not a problem. But it'd be great if you could water the plants around the pool a couple of times a week. There's a hose hooked up in back, near the diving board. That should take care of things until I have a chance to figure out what to do."

"Okay, sure," she agreed.

"Thanks, Megan," John said. "Honestly, I don't know what I'd do without you."

After she hung up, she sat at the island, thinking about how strangely still the house was. Silent, too, now that Endora had wandered off to another part of the house.

Then she remembered that this afternoon, her friends were coming over. She found herself looking forward to their visit with unusual eagerness. For reasons she couldn't explain, she suddenly felt very much alone here in John's house.

CHAPTER 15

To combat her lingering feelings of uneasiness, Megan got busy. She made coffee, filling the house with the intoxicating smell of Peet's French roast, then checked her email. After breakfast she took a long swim, followed by a steaming hot shower.

When she checked the time, she realized her friends were due shortly. She turned on loud music as she bustled around the kitchen, opening bags and jars, filling bowls, checking wine glasses for water spots. The crackers and pretzels left over from Greg's visit, the hunk of cheddar cheese, soda and wine . . . She arranged all the basics for successful entertaining around John's luxurious bouquet of yellow roses, prominently displayed in the center of the island.

Yet she was also aware of an uncomfortable tightness in her stomach. It was the result of knowing exactly how Brenda, Elissa, and Chloe felt about Greg—and what they were likely to say if they found out she'd seen him again.

She was still debating whether or not to even mention his reappearance when she heard the slamming of car doors. She stepped into the living room and saw that Brenda's red Accord had just pulled up in front of the house. A few seconds later, her three visitors were heading up the walkway, all of them lugging tote bags.

"You found me!" Megan called from the front door.

"Wowie-zowie!" Brenda cried as she swept inside. As usual, rather than simply walking into the room, she made a grand entrance, opening her arms so that her floor-length gold-and-black caftan swirled around her feet. "Have I died and gone to heaven?"

"You're *living* here?" Elissa showed considerably more reserve but was nevertheless breathless. "For *free?*"

Megan laughed. "That's what everyone says."

Everyone, she thought, being Greg.

"This place is amazing!" Chloe cooed. "And I haven't even gotten a look at that pool yet."

"You won't be disappointed," Megan assured her.

Endora chose that moment to make her own grand entrance. She trotted in from the hallway, meowing loudly.

"Who's this?" Elissa cried, crouching down.

"My roommate," Megan said. "Her name is Endora."

"What a sweetie!" Elissa, a self-pronounced cat person, had already swept the orange Maine coon into her arms and was nuzzling her fur.

"I'm becoming really fond of her," Megan admitted. "As far as I'm concerned, she's the best part of the deal."

"Uh, oh," Brenda teased. "Do I see a future cat-napping in the future?" She grimaced. "Cat-napping? Somehow that doesn't sound right . . . "

"How about a tour of the house?" Megan suggested.

"Something to drink first," Brenda insisted. "Then the tour."

"In that case, come into the kitchen," Megan said. "I'll point out some of the highlights on the way."

Her three friends ooh'd and ahh'd as they passed from the spacious living room through the dining room, then into the kitchen.

Elissa stopped dead in her tracks. "Wow! This is *fabulous!* It looks like a *restaurant* kitchen!"

"I saw one like this on the Home and Garden channel," Chloe said, her eyes wide. "If I lived here, I'd probably start baking bread or something."

"I haven't reached that point," Megan said. "But I do spend a lot of time in here."

"Hey, check these out," Brenda said, stopping in front of the vase of yellow long-stemmed roses. "Are these in our honor or are you just getting in the habit of spoiling yourself, now that you live in a mansion?"

"Actually, they were a gift," Megan said.

"Pretty fancy gift," Chloe commented.

"Who are they from?" Brenda asked. Her tone half-joking, she added, "An admirer?"

"Actually, they're from John," Megan replied, her voice strained. "The guy who owns the house."

"Wait a sec," Brenda said. "You're saying that not only does this guy let you live in his gorgeous house, free of charge, but he also showers you with gifts like expensive flowers?"

"What's so strange about that?" Megan asked, sounding defensive.

"If you ask me, he's got a thing for you," Brenda observed.

"We've already been through this." Megan rolled her eyes dramatically, not wanting to let on how disturbing she found her friends' teasing about John. "I think he just happens to be a really nice guy."

Anxious to steer the conversation away from John, she gestured toward the bottles on the island. "What would you like to drink?"

"Wine," Brenda replied. "Definitely wine. The whole point of Sundays is that you don't have to wait for a respectable time like five o'clock to start drinking."

As her friends settled in around the island, Megan poured wine for everyone.

"A toast," she said, holding up her glass. "I want to thank all of you for coming over today. It really means a lot to me."

"To friendship!" Elissa cried, clinking her glass against Megan's.

"How about a toast to life as a kept woman?" Brenda suggested with a grin.

Megan rolled her eyes. "Hardly. More like the hired help."

"Honestly, Megan," Elissa said seriously, "we're all really happy you found this place. You deserve a chance to regroup."

"Here, here," Chloe seconded, holding her glass in the air once again. "How about a toast to our charming hostess?"

They clinked their glasses again. Then silence fell over the group as they all sipped their wine.

It was Megan who broke the silence. "It's so great to see all of you," she said sincerely. "So tell me: what's been going on? I feel like I've been totally out of the loop."

She listened eagerly as Elissa filled her in on the latest gossip from work and Chloe entertained them all with a hilarious tale of her last audition—which turned out to be for a TV commercial for a laxative.

"What about you, Megan?" Brenda asked, bringing the conversation back to her. "How are you enjoying living here?"

Megan hesitated, wondering how honest to be. "It's great," she finally replied. "I mean, look at how much space I've got all to myself."

"What about living alone?" Elissa asked, sounding concerned. "Are you getting used to it?"

"Pretty much." Megan could hear the hollowness of her own voice.

"Are we your first visitors?" Chloe asked.

Megan hesitated before answering. "Not exactly."

Brenda's eyebrows shot up. "Now *that* sounds mysterious. Don't tell me I was right, and that you've already hooked up with some wealthy gentleman here in Pasadena."

"Not quite." As casually as she could, Megan said, "Greg stopped by on Friday night."

"*What?*" Brenda shrieked.

"Oh, my!" Chloe cried. "I can't believe you just dropped that into the conversation like it was nothing!"

"I wasn't sure if I should mention it at all," Megan admitted.

"So how is good old Greg?" Brenda asked dryly.

"He seems fine."

"I knew I shouldn't have told him you were housesitting," Elissa said. "He's probably hoping you'll invite him to move in with you."

"Actually, I was pretty surprised to hear from him," Megan said. "I'm still not sure what it was about."

"He wants something," Brenda said, nodding wisely. "Mark my words."

"What he probably wants is to get Megan back," Elissa said.

"Of course he wants her back!" Chloe agreed. Turning to Megan, she added, "You're the best thing that ever happened to him. Even he's sharp enough to get that."

"When it comes to Greg," Brenda said, "I've got one piece of advice: just say no. Hey, can I get a refill on the wine?"

"Of course," Megan said, glad she'd changed the subject. "Now how about that tour of the house?"

Wine glasses in hand, the four of them filed out of the kitchen. Megan had already decided that she'd take them to the pool through the French doors, showing off the house's crowning glory with as much drama as possible.

"I can't wait to show you the master bedroom," she said, leading the way along the carpeted corridor. "That's where I'm staying. And I have to show you the amazing bathroom. You won't believe the Jacuzzi tub . . ."

"What's in here?" Brenda demanded. She'd stopped in front of John's office, grabbing hold of the doorknob and rattling it noisily. "Hey, this room is locked!"

"That's right," Megan said. "That's John's office. He keeps all his important stuff locked up in there."

Brenda screwed up her face, as if in disbelief. "Or else he's one of those guys who's into kinky stuff and he's got a dungeon in there!"

"He works from home," Megan explained patiently. "He does stuff with computers. Apparently he has access to a lot of information that his company doesn't want anybody else to get hold of."

"Sounds like he's a spy," Chloe commented.

"He works for a company called Kerwood Industries," Megan said.

Elissa frowned. "Kerwood Industries? I've never heard of it. Is it here in Pasadena?"

"I don't know where it is," Megan admitted. "But since he works from home, I guess it could be anywhere."

"What does the company do?" Chloe asked.

"I don't know that, either," Megan said.

"You're certainly a trusting soul!" Brenda exclaimed.

Megan blinked. "What do you mean, trusting?"

"Here you move into a total stranger's house," Brenda replied, "without knowing anything about him. Who he is, what he does . . . And he's got a room that's locked up like Fort Knox and you don't even know what's in it."

"He told me what's in it," Megan said, her patience running out. "Files and computers and other work-related stuff."

Brenda's eyes widened. "Maybe he lied. Maybe he's growing pot with those special plant lights, and one of these days there's going to be a police raid and you're going to end up in prison!"

"Or maybe it's even worse," Chloe said. "Maybe he's got a crystal meth lab in there."

Brenda nodded knowingly. "Which would explain how he can afford a place like this."

"Or maybe it really is a dungeon." Chloe's big blue eyes grew round. "Stone walls, whips and chains . . ."

"Or guns!" Elissa cried. "Maybe he has an arsenal in there. He could even be one of those survivalists who thinks the world's coming to an end."

"In that case it'd be well-stocked with canned goods and bottled water," Brenda said, feigning seriousness. "Nice to know you're in good shape, just in case the world really does come to an end." Glaring at the closed door, she added, "Of course, you'd have to bang down the door first."

"Chill, Brenda," Megan said, her tone sharper than she intended. While Brenda's bigger-than-life personality was usually refreshing, at the moment she was finding her a bit trying.

Brenda didn't seem to notice. "Hey, I've got an idea!" she said. "Let's look for the key!"

"Look, John trusts me," Megan insisted, tired of these ridiculous speculations. "I'm not going to go prowling around the one place he doesn't want me to go!"

"Where's your spirit of adventure?" Brenda demanded. "I say we do a full-scale search. I'm not leaving until I know what's in that room!"

"Give it up, Bren," Elissa said with a sigh. "I don't know about you, but I'm dying to see the rest of the house."

"I'll show you my room," Megan offered, more than happy to change their focus. "It's down here, at the end of the hall."

As soon as they stepped through the doorway, Elissa and Chloe murmured their approval. But Brenda stepped ahead of them, into the middle of the room.

"So this is the master bedroom, huh?" Rubbing her hands together greedily, she added, "It looks like John left a lot of his stuff behind—which makes this our big chance to know the man of the house a little better!"

"You're not doing any snooping," Megan insisted. She was beginning to regret taking them on this tour.

But Brenda was already opening dresser drawers. "Ooh, check this out!" she cried. "The man really is a neat freak! Which isn't necessarily a *bad* thing . . ."

Before Megan had a chance to tell her to stop, she caught a glimpse inside the shirt drawer. Just like before, the pale green polo shirt stood out among the subdued shades of blue and brown. But while she could have sworn she remembered it as being crooked, this time its edges appeared to be neatly aligned with all the others.

But she forgot all about her puzzlement when Chloe announced, "I didn't come here to go through some guy's sock drawer. I want to go swimming!"

Elissa, who had drifted over to the French doors, let out an appreciative gasp. "Wow, check out that pool! Megan, where can we change?"

After her friends left, Megan energetically collected the empty wineglasses and sponged crumbs off the counter, fueled by an adrenaline rush. Their delight over the house reinforced her own enthusiasm for her temporary home, and she found even the simple act of cleaning up a pleasure.

Yet something nagged at her. As hard as she tried to discount Brenda's reservations, she couldn't keep her friends' comments from playing through her head.

"Here you move into a total stranger's house, without knowing anything about him. Who he is, what he does . . ."

She decided to do a little more poking around. Only this time, it wasn't John's dresser drawers she was going to check out. As soon as she finished straightening up, she sat down at the island and turned on her laptop. She clicked keys until the Google home page came up, then typed in the key words "John Davis."

She let out a cry of surprise when more than 36 million listings come up. The first page alone listed the websites of a movie producer, a business consultant, a weightlifter, and an artist, as well as a few websites about an English explorer from the 1500s and an American politician and diplomat who died in 1955.

She realized she was foolish to have assumed researching such a common name would be easy. She thought for a few seconds, then typed in the key word "prednisone."

Most of the websites that came up looked credible. But she clicked on the National Institute of Health's, figuring it was likely to have the most accurate information.

What she read did little to satisfy her curiosity about John. Prednisone, she learned, was a steroid—a corticosteroid, whatever that meant—used for a long list of illnesses, from arthritis and allergies to lupus and multiple sclerosis. It was also used to treat cancer and pneumonia that was associated with AIDS.

She read the entire page, absorbing everything there was to know about prednisone. Yet the most interesting thing she learned was that John most likely had some ailment as commonplace as arthritis.

She shut her laptop, chastising herself for actually being disappointed that she didn't find out some deep dark secret about John Davis. As she toddled off to bed, she felt a little smug that when it came to the possibility of her benefactor having a dark side, she was right and Brenda was wrong.

CHAPTER 16

There's something about Mondays, Megan thought as she sipped her breakfast coffee, that makes you want to rush right out and put everything in your life in order.

Or maybe the reason she was feeling especially energized was that she was finally becoming accustomed to living in John's house. She looked around the kitchen, marveling over the fact that she'd only been here since Thursday afternoon. Already she'd fallen into a routine.

And it wasn't just her everyday responsibilities, like feeding Endora. It was mastering the coffeepot and all the other small appliances and knowing where to find the colander, the sugar bowl, the plate with the different colored stripes she particularly liked. It was coming out of the shower and knowing exactly where to reach for the towel. It was hearing a noise—the hum of the refrigerator, a creak of the floorboards—and being able to identify it immediately. The evening before, she'd found the hose and watered the plants surrounding the pool. She moved around the property with the confidence of someone who really lived there, plucking out the occasional weed and speculating about how the rock garden could be reconfigured.

She was really starting to feel at home.

It was a wonderful sensation, one she hadn't experienced since she'd left Pennsylvania. Los Angeles had felt like a place where she was destined to remain an outsider, someone who never really belonged. But now, all that had changed.

She was also fascinated by how much she was learning about the house's owner, simply by sharing his living space. The fact that John didn't like spicy food, for example, as evidenced by the absence of any condiments more interesting than salt, pepper, and an ancient jar of mild salsa languishing at the back of the refrigerator. She'd also noticed his preference for unscented products, like the laundry soap he bought, no doubt because of the allergies that were responsible for his Singulaire prescription.

It's interesting how well you can get to know someone by living in their house, she thought.

Even more importantly, she'd worked out the intricacies of keeping Endora happy and well fed. As she sat at the kitchen island, the furry orange pussycat lay curled up in her lap, seemingly the picture of contentment. She was certainly purring as if she was in a state of pure bliss, even though Megan only stroked her sporadically. She was much more focused on typing on the laptop in front of her.

She scooped Endora up in one arm then stood up and stretched. The cat meowed loudly, telling her in no uncertain terms that she wanted to get down. Reluctantly, Megan complied. Endora, she realized, had become her security blanket, her teddy bear, and the best roommate she'd ever had. Always there to keep her company, never complaining, never stealing her food or borrowing her clothes.

But as comfortable as she'd become here at the house, she was ready to make a foray out into the world that would help her advance her goal of finding a job. She rinsed out her breakfast dishes and headed for the shower, already constructing a mental to-do list.

Despite its reputation as a stodgy suburb, Pasadena had a lively downtown area. Shops and restaurants lined the two main streets that formed an L, South Lake and Colorado Boulevard. Chain stores, largely, but with enough of the character of the city's earlier incarnations remaining that Megan still enjoyed poking around.

East Colorado morphed into a funkier section. The wide street was lined with ethnic restaurants, a multiplex theater specializing in foreign movies and independent films, and a fabulous bookstore, Vroman's, where she'd spent many hours. In fact, whenever Megan fantasized about being a writer one day, she pictured a display in Vroman's window, with stacks of her books and a big poster announcing her upcoming talk and book-signing.

Today, however, she was all business as she went into the bookstore, skipping the enticing displays of new titles and the endless aisles just waiting to be perused.

Instead, she asked the first clerk she spotted where she could find books on writing résumés. She spent almost half an hour considering each one, then chose two she thought would enable her to put the finishing touches on the draft she'd written.

She was about to get back in her car when she spotted Speedy's, just a few doors down from where she'd parked. She now felt a special kinship with the place, since that was where her housesitting gig had started. She realized that Speedy's could help her get her life in shape in other ways, as well.

She went inside and studied the list of printing services hanging on the wall. She'd noticed it every time she'd gone in, but never paid much attention to it before.

"Anything I can help you with?" the young man behind the counter asked.

He was considerably younger than she was, with the look of a college student. Jet-black hair that thanks to an abundance of gel flipped up in front, giving him a punk look. Multiple facial piercings. Ripped jeans and a black T-shirt, probably to show off the elaborate tattoos that crawled across both arms.

"I'm putting together a résumé," she said, still scanning the list behind him. "I want it to look really professional."

He nodded. "We can take care of that. I'd go with the offset printing, maybe on a textured ivory stock."

She was surprised he knew so much. "How much would that cost?"

"How many copies?"

"I don't know," she replied. "Maybe a hundred?"

Before he had a chance to answer, the telephone on the wall behind him rang. She braced herself, expecting she'd have to wait while he answered. Instead, he pulled out a loose-leaf notebook and flipped through the lists of prices.

The phone continued to ring.

"It's okay if you get that," she told him. "I can wait."

He grimaced. "If I answered the phone every time it rang, I'd never get a thing done. I'll let it go to voicemail."

He continued to ignore it as he ran his finger along a laminated page, then quoted her a price.

"Okay, great," she said, nodding. "I'll be back as soon as it's ready."

It was nearly noon by the time she got home. Megan headed for the refrigerator, smiling at the realization that she, like Endora, ate by the clock. At the moment, all she could focus on was whether her luncheon entrée should be yogurt or cheese.

She opened the refrigerator, picturing the shelves inside stocked with the few items she'd bought at Trader Joe's. So she did a double take when her eyes zoomed in on something that didn't belong.

Lying on the bottom shelf was a green bottle that she readily identified as champagne. Moet et Chandon in fact, her favorite brand.

CHAPTER 17

Megan took the champagne out of the refrigerator, as if she needed to touch the bottle's cold, hard surface to be completely convinced that it was real. Just holding it in her hands sent a chill through her—a reaction she suspected wasn't the least bit related to the bottle's iciness.

This is too strange, she thought, swallowing hard. What could this possibly be about?

But while she had no idea what a bottle of champagne was doing in her refrigerator, there was one thing that was disturbingly clear: someone else had been in the house.

She was still staring at the bottle, trying to comprehend what was going on, when her cell phone rang.

"Hello?" she answered, her voice reflecting her distractedness.

"Hey, Megan. It's John."

"Hi, John," she said wearily.

"Just called to see how everything's going." Sounding a bit anxious, he added, "I don't want to be a bother, but I figured that you're still getting used to the place and that you might have some questions."

"Actually," she said, trying not to let on how upset she was, "something kind of odd just happened."

When he didn't respond, she continued, "A bottle of champagne magically appeared in the refrigerator."

More silence. Then he finally said, "It's a present. My way of saying thanks for looking after Endora and the house."

So it's from John, she thought with relief. Yet she was still confused.

"But how did it get there?" she asked.

Another moment of silence before he said, "It was supposed to be a delightful surprise. The cleaning people put it there. I asked them to."

"You definitely surprised me," she said, her tone harsher than she intended. "I wasn't aware that anyone else had access to the house."

Sounding apologetic, he said, "I can't believe I forgot to tell you I have a cleaning service."

"You probably should have mentioned that." Now that the mystery had been solved, she was unable to conceal her irritation.

"I know," John said, a trifle breathless. "I'm so sorry. I totally forgot. They have a key and our usual routine is that they just let themselves in without even ringing the bell, so I don't even think about when they're coming. Even if I'm at home, sitting at my computer, they work around me. I'm barely even aware they're in the house. Anyway, I asked them to pick up a bottle of champagne for you, but I didn't know when they'd actually deliver it."

"What days do they come?" Megan walked over to the refrigerator and took down the stapled sheets, ready to write down the information.

"We don't have a set schedule," John replied. "They fit me in around their other clients. It's the arrangement we worked out. I don't really care when they show up, and they knock something off the price because I'm willing to be flexible."

Sighing, she set the papers down on the counter. "How often do they come?"

"Every couple of weeks or so, depending. But like I say, I don't really keep track of their comings and goings. They send me a bill once a month and I mail them a check."

Terrific, she thought grimly. From now on, I can't even walk from the shower into the bedroom without putting on a robe. For all I know, I'll come waltzing out of the bathroom and find some guy with a vacuum cleaner standing there.

She told herself that it was a small price to pay for free housing. And a heated pool.

And Endora.

She found that she couldn't quite muster up her usual enthusiasm.

"Well, thanks for telling me," she said, trying to sound more upbeat than she felt. "And thanks for the champagne."

"You're welcome." John's voice was thick with remorse as he added, "I'm really sorry it freaked you out. I was trying to be—I don't know, spontaneous and fun. And I figured everybody likes champagne."

She was starting to feel bad about being so harsh. After all, he was only trying to be nice.

"I do like champagne," she told him. "In fact, I'm afraid I'm a bit of a champagne snob. Moet et Chandon happens to be my favorite."

"No kidding," he replied, sounding relieved. "Look, I just wanted you to know how much I appreciate you. The fact that you're taking care of my house and my cat and all."

"So far, this seems to be working out pretty well for both of us," she agreed.

"I'm glad you feel that way," he said. "Frankly, I thank my lucky stars every day that I'm stuck out here in Minneapolis that you came along to bail me out of what was looking like an impossible situation.

"And speaking of being stuck in Minneapolis, I'd better get back to work," he added heartily. "I should really be doing what they sent me here to do."

"Have a good week," she said.

But as soon as she hung up, Megan ran through the past few days in her mind. She realized that in the past five days, since she moved into John's house, he'd called her every single day. She was debating whether to feel annoyed or flattered.

Maybe he doesn't trust me, the way he says he does, she thought. Or maybe my friends are right about him being interested in me.

Who knows? Maybe at some point we'll become something more than a homeowner with a cat and his housesitter. Instead of feeling optimistic about that possibility, or even amused, she found the thought oddly disturbing.

There's something about John that's . . . unsettling, she thought. She decided she was glad he was fifteen hundred miles away.

She made up her mind to go for a swim, since it was the best way of clearing her mind. She headed into her bedroom, anxious to change into a bathing suit and get into the water. But first she went into the bathroom to use the toilet.

As she was washing her hands, she looked past her reflection in the mirror and noticed something squiggly on the wall inside the shower. It was shiny, reflecting the light.

Frowning, Megan turned around and opened the glass door to see what it was.

It was her honeysuckle shower gel, she discovered, running her finger through it and sniffing it. It must have dripped down when she was showering earlier this morning, before she went out.

Some cleaning service, she thought as she closed the shower door. Or maybe I misunderstood. Maybe John asked them to drop off the champagne whenever it was convenient, even if it wasn't one of their cleaning days.

I certainly hope so, she thought. Otherwise, he sure isn't getting his money's worth.

She made a mental note to mention it to him the next time they talked, then quickly scrapped the idea. Stuck out in Minneapolis, far away from home, the last thing he needed was something else to worry about. Besides, she didn't want to sound as if she was a complainer. Especially since he was trying so hard to be nice.

Yet deep down, she was starting to admit that between John's intrusiveness and all the other disturbing things that had happened since she moved in, this housesitting gig wasn't turning out quite the way she expected. In fact, she was starting to feel as if maybe having John's trip turn out to be shorter than they'd both anticipated wouldn't be such a bad thing.

CHAPTER 18

That afternoon, as Megan sat by the pool with her laptop, she tried to focus on the positives of living in John's house instead of fretting about the negatives. She looked around the backyard, taking in the glistening turquoise water of the pool, the open French doors, the filmy white curtains undulating in the light afternoon breeze . . .

She jumped at the sound of a car door slamming.

It sounded close. Close enough to be coming from the driveway.

She braced herself, pretty sure of who it was likely to be. So she wasn't the least bit surprised when a few seconds later, Greg sauntered through the back gate, his self-confident grin lighting up his face.

"Well, well. Look what the cat dragged in," she greeted him. She remained seated, offering him only a weak smile.

"Hey, Megs!" He sauntered over to her, his hands jammed in the front pockets of his khaki shorts. "How's it going?"

"Great," she replied, still guarded. "So . . . what brings you all the way out here?"

"I unexpectedly found myself with a free afternoon." He lowered himself into the white wrought-iron chair opposite hers and folded his hands over his bright Hawaiian shirt. "So I thought I'd stop by to see how you're doing."

She studied him warily, wishing she had the ability to translate what he was saying.

"I'm in the mood for a movie," he continued. "Want to come?"

"Greg, I really should—"

"Come on, Megs. We'll only be gone a couple of hours." Glancing around the yard, he added, "You don't want to turn into a hermit, do you? There's more to life than hanging around the house, even a really fancy one."

"Sure," she said, finding the idea of getting out of the house for a while appealing.

"Great!" he said. "There's a theater near here that shows classic films. We can just make the three o'clock showing of *Rear Window*. The classic Hitchcock film? James Stewart, Grace Kelly?"

"I'm ready," she said, closing her laptop. "All I have to do is lock up the house."

Megan found it difficult to concentrate on the movie. She was too aware of Greg sitting next to her in the dark. It didn't take long for her to regret coming with him, putting herself in a situation she hadn't expected to be in ever again. She was worried that she was letting herself get roped into something she knew, deep down, she wanted no part of.

Afterward, Greg suggested getting something to eat. Her first impulse was to say no, but she realized she was hungry.

We'll just grab something quick, she told herself. You'll be back home before you know it.

As they sat opposite each other at a Chinese restaurant, once again Greg did most of the talking. Yet this time around, she was glad. She was trying to put as little effort into this as possible, the best way she knew of remaining detached.

This is about steamed dumplings and chicken with cashews, she told herself. Nothing more. But then, when their plates were almost empty, Greg folded his arms and placed them on the table in front of him.

"Actually," he said seriously, his luminescent blue eyes fixed on hers, "I have an ulterior motive for coming to Pasadena today. There's something I've been dying to talk to you about."

Megan's stomach sank for reasons that had nothing to do with all the Chinese food she'd just eaten. The sinking feeling worsened when he announced, "I've come up with a million dollar idea."

"Greg," she began, holding up both hands as if she could fight off his words. But he ignored her.

"You know how everybody's obsessed with taking videos of practically their entire lives these days," he asked, "then putting them on websites like YouTube?"

She hesitated, then nodded.

"And you know how at college graduation ceremonies, one of the highlights is always a montage of candid shots from the past four years—frat parties and Homecoming and all that?"

"Yes . . ."

"Okay, so here's my idea." He paused, his blue eyes shining. "Starting a company that takes videos of a kid throughout his four years of college and, at the end, puts together a DVD that's just of him and his friends—or her—that captures their entire college experience."

She was silent for a few seconds, digesting what she'd just heard.

"Greg, I think that's an amazing idea." Her praise was sincere. In fact, she could hardly believe that he'd finally come up with something that sounded as if it might actually work.

"I've already thought up a name for it: U-Tube," he went on, his voice becoming more and more animated. "That's the letter 'u.', for university, instead of 'you'."

"Got it," she said. "And I like it."

He sat back in his seat, beaming. "It's inspired, right? I figure I'll have reps at all the college orientation programs. Students, probably, manning a table along with all the other businesses that try to get kids to sign on right at the beginning of their freshman year. Cell phone plans, credit cards . . . even ski resorts go to those sometimes, selling season passes at a student rate. I'll start with UCLA, then hire students to work for me at other colleges in L.A., like USC and Caltech.

"I've even got a guy who's willing to go in on it with me," he added. "A business partner, a guy who's a financial wizard. I'm serious about this, Megs. I really think it could take off."

Megan could hardly believe what she was hearing. It's actually a good idea, she thought, amazed. Something that could really work. And for once, Greg seems to have thought it all out.

When he drove her back to the house, he pulled up in front, letting the motor run.

"It was good to see you," he said, keeping his eyes on the dashboard.

"It was fun," she admitted. She was surprised, not only by how different he seemed tonight, but also by the fact that she really had enjoyed herself.

He sounded uncharacteristically bashful as he added, "I was thinking . . ."

"Yes?"

"Maybe I'll come over again tomorrow night. We could go to another movie or something."

Megan's head felt clouded. But even though she yearned for time to think about what was happening here, she heard herself say, "Sure. That sounds fun."

"Cool," he said.

And then he leaned over and kissed her lightly on the lips. Even though they'd kissed thousands of times before, this kiss sent a jolt of electricity through her.

She still felt shaky once she was inside. She scooped Endora up into her arms, expecting that being back at home would calm her. Instead, she was struck by how quiet the house was. And how horribly lonely it felt to be wandering through its empty rooms all by herself.

CHAPTER 19

The *intruder is back.* He stands outside the house, his fists clenched, his mouth drawn into a thin line as he watches. His entire body gripped by an anger that's so strong he can't see past it. It's almost as if he's shrouded in total darkness.

And then another feeling pushes through, gnawing at him so strongly it threatens to devour him. A craving. The feeling of wanting something so badly he knows he'll do whatever it takes to have it.

The same way it was with Caroline.

He never intended to hurt her. He simply wanted to have her all to himself, to possess someone who lived only for him.

Caroline was pretty, too.

With her golden hair and green eyes, she hadn't looked at all like Megan. Still, Caroline was like her in so many other ways. So sweet. So trusting.

And he'd been so certain that he sensed something rare in her: the ability to truly care about someone, to make that person the center of her universe.

Luring her into the barn had been easy. She was a whole year younger than he was, a grade behind him at school, so she looked up to him. She seemed flattered when he invited her to come see the new kittens he told her were inside.

At first, when she saw what was happening, Caroline was afraid. But that was to be expected. The heavy padlock on the barn doors, the ropes he used to tie her up . . . it wasn't surprising that she felt as if she was his prisoner, at first.

But he didn't lose heart. Not when he knew he could convince her to trust him. And to make her understand that all they needed was each other. He kept telling her he didn't want to hurt her. That all he wanted was a friend, just like the other kids had.

He'd treated her so well. Bringing her blankets and pillows, books to read, toys to play with, stuffed animals. Food, too, even special treats like candy.

Everything she needed to be happy.

He was so considerate, so careful to fill every one of her needs. And he asked so little in return. All he wanted was for her to care about him the way he cared about her.

And she'd pretended to, after that first day. He'd actually believed that she'd come to accept him and her new life.

Until the third morning, when she'd woken up screaming.

He hadn't liked hurting her. It wasn't even the feeling of the pocketknife's dull blade cutting through her skin that had bothered him. It was watching its creamy whiteness turn red, hearing her cries of pain muffled by the rag he'd stuffed in her mouth and fastened with duct tape.

She has to learn, he'd thought, forcing himself to go on. She has to stop resisting, give me more time.

Eventually she'll come around.

She'd quieted down after that. At least for another day.

Then, once he was convinced that she'd finally understood that this was how things were going to be from now on, he tried to kiss her. Never expecting that she'd turn into an animal, kicking and scratching and doing everything she could to hurt him.

They'd fought. He never would have guessed she was so strong. So determined.

Or that she'd grab the glass bottle of juice he'd brought when she'd asked for it. The single blow to his head had stunned him, just for a few seconds.

Long enough for her to escape.

He hadn't anticipated that she would run away, that she'd be fast enough and agile enough to squeeze through the narrow space between the two barn doors.

He hadn't anticipated that she would tell, either.

He'd tried desperately to explain to everyone that all he'd ever wanted was for the two of them to make each other happy. But no one listened. Not his mother, who kept crying and saying she didn't know what she'd done wrong. Not his father, who grew angry and said he wasn't the least bit surprised he'd turned out this way. Not even the psychologists and social workers who acted like they wanted to be his friend.

No one heard him. Instead, he was sent to The Lost Place. Driven in a van with bars on the windows. No heat, even though the temperature outside dipped below zero and dirty snow coated the countryside.

Handcuffs chafing against his pale skin. Shackles rooting his feet to the floor. He thought that finally getting there would be a relief. Until he saw it.

A three-story cinderblock building, the same dull gray as the snow. Rising out of the ground in the middle of nowhere, at the end of a bumpy winding road. Thick bars on the windows, barbed wire curling over the top of the tall iron fence.

The inside even worse.

No soft surfaces, only hard. Metal, cinderblock, concrete. Squared off edges, stark angular shapes. But the ugliness wasn't the worst part. The counselors, either. Or the regimentation.

At twelve, he was one of the youngest.

That in itself would have made him a target. But his delicate features and thin frame made him even more vulnerable.

Jeers. Insults. Punches the counselors never saw, towels snapped hard in the shower, cartons of milk poured over his lunch.

None of it compared to that one night.

He finds himself drifting back there one more time, replaying it in his head.

Reliving it as if it were actually happening, all over again.

It's late, after hours. All the lights are out. Everyone is in bed. Or supposed to be. He's lying awake, hating everything about his life, when the door swings open.

They rush inside, not wanting to be seen. Three of them.

He can still hear their taunting voices. Hoarse whispers, soft enough that none of the counselors can hear, loud enough that he doesn't miss a single word.

Even in the darkness, he can see their faces, looming over him as he lies in bed, not moving. All three of them smirking as one of them, the biggest boy, whispers, "You sure look like a girl!" And then, glancing over his shoulder at the others: "So let's see if you're as good as one."

He never gets that night out of his head. It's with him always, the fear, the humiliation, the pain.

With it, the conviction that he'll never let that happen again.

A lot of time has passed since then. And he's done a good job of blending in. Hiding from his past, making sure no one ever found out.

Yet the same urge that sent him to The Lost Place never left. The all-consuming need for someone to love, someone who's capable of returning what he's so ready to give. He's simply been waiting for the right situation. And the right person.

Someone like Megan.

The right time, too. Not yet, of course. It's still too soon.

But he's bursting with impatience. He can't wait to start learning everything there is to know about her. What she eats, when she sleeps, where she goes, who she sees.

To be close enough to hear her voice on the phone, her footsteps on the carpet. Even to hear her breathe.

Staying on the outside, lurking around the edges of her life, is no longer enough.

He knows exactly what he has to do.

He closes his eyes and pictures the basement. Cringing as he imagines what it will be like to spend so much time in the dark, enclosed space.

Still, he has to do it.

With Caroline, he messed up. Hardly surprising, since he was still a kid.

This time, he's determined to get it right. And with Megan, everything should go exactly the way he wants.

After all, she's already living in his house.

CHAPTER 20

Tuesday evening, as Megan dressed for her evening with Greg, she couldn't help being a bundle of nerves.

The third date, she thought, studying her reflection in the bathroom mirror. Everybody knows what that means.

It's not a date, she reminded herself. Not even close. It's just a movie, a chance to get out of the house. Still, she spent too much time deciding what to wear and fussing with her hair. When she put on her makeup, she chastised herself for not replacing her lost lipstick.

It's got to be here somewhere, she told herself, cross over having been so careless. It didn't just walk away.

She was about to get down on the floor and take another look when the doorbell rang. She ran her fingers through her hair one last time, then made a point of walking, not running, to the front door.

"Hey," she greeted Greg calmly after throwing open the door.

"Hey, yourself," he said, grinning.

He leaned forward and gave her a peck on the cheek before she had a chance to dodge him. She told herself it was barely even a kiss, that it was simply the type of greeting people give each other all the time.

Be careful, a voice inside her head warned.

"Come on in," she said, moving aside. "Can I get you something to drink?"

He rubbed his hands together. "What have you got?"

"Just wine."

"Perfect."

They sat side-by-side at the kitchen island, their stemmed glasses in front of them.

"So what do you want to do tonight?" she asked. "I can go online and look for a movie—"

"Actually," Greg said, "I feel like staying in."

"Okay," she said, uncertain of what he really meant. "In that case, do you want to sit outside, next to the pool?"

"Sure," he said.

They grabbed their glasses and the wine bottle and headed outside through the back door. The moon was round and bright, the centerpiece of a star-splattered sky. The air was cool, and Megan wished she'd thrown on a jacket. Instead she hugged herself to keep warm.

She walked over to the table and chairs. Greg followed, but after depositing his glass and the bottle there, he headed for the pool. He pulled off his sneakers and plopped down at the edge, dangling his bare feet in the water.

"This is nice," he said, glancing up at her. "You should try it."

She hesitated, not sure if this was a good idea. But in the end she kicked off her sandals and sat down next to him.

"The water feels great," he commented.

"It really does," she agreed.

He turned to face her, grinning. "Hey, I've got an idea. How about a moonlight swim?"

Once again, she hesitated. Then: "Sure. Might as well take advantage of the pool."

"There's one problem, though," he said. "I didn't bring a suit."

She wondered if she could find a men's bathing suit in a drawer, one that John left behind. Then decided that borrowing his clothes would be overstepping a few boundaries.

Instead, she suggested, "You could swim in your underwear."

"Or I could go skinny-dipping." He smiled flirtatiously. "You could, too."

"Oh. Well." She could feel the heat rising on her cheeks, and she was glad it was dark enough that he couldn't see her blushing. "It's kind of cool out here."

"Hey, the pool's heated, right? The water feels amazing!"

She laughed nervously. "Even so, I think I'll wear a bathing suit."

He shrugged, then pulled himself up, already unbuttoning his shirt. While Megan had seen him without his clothes more times than she could count, she looked away, suddenly shy.

"I'll go inside and change," she said, hopping up. "Be right back."

She went back into the house, but this time used the French doors. She flipped on the light, instantly realizing that Greg could undoubtedly see her through the filmy white curtains. She grabbed her turquoise two-piece suit and stepped into the bathroom.

She was back outside less than two minutes later.

"Hey," Greg greeted her, watching her cross the patio. "I missed you."

She smiled uneasily, not sure how to respond. She was glad that he was already in the water, submerged so that only his head was visible.

As she neared the pool, she lowered her head, pretending to study the water. She glanced at the diving board, but decided not to make such a dramatic entrance. Instead, she crouched down at the deep end and slipped in.

Instead of feeling relaxed in the water, however, she was uncomfortable. Being in the pool with Greg, bathed in moonlight, created an unexpected feeling of intimacy.

She treaded water, staying a good eight or ten feet away from him.

"Doesn't this feel great?" he asked. "This was a good idea, right?"

"It's wonderful," she agreed, her voice prim.

"Hey, wanna get up on my shoulders?"

"That's okay."

"C'mon," he insisted. "You didn't used to be such a wuss."

His reference to their past, however vague, irritated her. But before she could protest again, he was swimming toward her, his broad shoulders dipping in and out of the water. Before she could move away, he grabbed her around her waist. The feeling of his hands on her was startling at first, but it was only a second or two before it felt comfortably familiar.

"I'll go under and you climb onto my shoulders," he instructed.

"Sitting or standing?" she asked, stalling.

Their faces were only inches apart, and she could smell the alcohol on his breath. She wiped away the drops of water on her cheeks, using her hands to put up a barrier between them.

She was relieved when he replied, "Standing. Then you can jump into the water. I'll be your human diving board!"

He dived under the surface, his hair momentarily floating on top like an undulating sea creature. Then he crouched on the bottom. She held onto his head as she placed one foot, then the other, on his shoulders.

She'd barely gotten into place before he abruptly sprang upward, thrusting her high into the air.

"Ah-h-h-h!" she screamed, part fearful, part delighted.

It was exhilarating, rising up out of the water like that. She was suspended for only a second or two, high above the water, before she felt herself losing her balance. And then she was plunging downward, unable to control her fall, the water swooshing around her ears as she sank into it.

She swam to the surface and poked her head out, gasping for breath.

"Cool, huh?" Greg exclaimed, looking triumphant.

"That was really fun," she agreed, still breathless as she swiped at her eyes and ran her fingers through her hair, pushing it out of her face. "I haven't done that since I was a little kid."

"Want to do it again?"

"I think I need to get back to that wine," she said.

She was already making her way to the edge. What was supposed to be simply fun had ended up being much more, and she wasn't sure she wanted to repeat it.

"Aw, c'mon," he protested.

But he didn't try to stop her as she climbed out of the pool. Instead, he swam to the edge and lifted himself out. Megan, already standing on the patio, watched the muscles of his water-splattered shoulders and back as they tensed. He had followed her suggestion, wearing his briefs and nothing else. Now that they were wet, they clung to him, revealing large patches of his skin.

Somewhere deep inside, she felt a twinge of what she recognized as desire. She immediately forced herself to push it away.

"So what about that wine?" he asked, rubbing his hands together.

Unlike her, he didn't seem bothered by the chill in the autumn air. She'd wrapped her arms around her middle again, pretending it was because of the coolness. But she also felt vulnerable in her two-piece bathing suit, which suddenly seemed alarming small.

"Let's go back inside," she said, briskly rubbing her stomach and hopping up and down.

"Okay," he agreed.

He scooped up both glasses in one hand and the wine bottle in the other. But instead of moving toward the back door, he made a beeline for the French doors.

Megan had no choice but to follow.

Once inside the bedroom, they both blinked in the bright light. Megan stood awkwardly in the middle of the room, aware of the tension that had followed them inside. She watched as Greg put the bottle and the glasses on the table next to the bed, then sat down on the edge.

"I'm all wet," he apologized. "Sorry about that."

"That's okay," she said quickly.

"Hey, you're freezing!" he observed.

She was, indeed, shivering, although she still wasn't sure it was only from the combination of wet skin and the chilly October night.

"Come over here," he commanded. "I'll warm you up."

"Greg," she said hesitantly.

And then she stiffened, a reaction that had nothing to do with either Greg or how cold she was.

"Wait. Did you hear something?" she asked, her voice breathless. For reasons she couldn't explain, she felt as if her stomach had just dropped to the floor.

Greg laughed. "Only the beat, beat, beat of my heart."

"No, seriously," she said. "Like a door shutting. Like—like the house shaking, just a little."

"C'mon, Megs," he said, his voice now soft. "Relax. It's me."

"Sorry," she said sheepishly. "I guess I'm just a little nervous."

When he walked over to her and enveloped her in a bear hug, she tensed up again. But he swung her gently from side to side in what seemed like a brotherly gesture.

"Is that helping?" he asked.

"I guess."

"Hey," he suddenly said, his voice husky, "I just had another great idea."

"What?"

"Let's check out that Jacuzzi you told me about. Where is it?"

"Right in there," she replied, pointing even though he couldn't see her hand. "In the bathroom."

"Sweet. Let's go warm you up."

He released her and started across the room. Megan's heart was pounding as she debated the wisdom of what she was considering.

But the fact that she followed him meant she'd already made up her mind.

Inside the bathroom, Greg leaned over and turned on both faucets. A violent stream of water cascaded down, filling the huge tub quickly.

"Got any bubbles?" he asked, standing up straight and facing her.

Megan laughed. "I doubt it. A guy lives here."

"Too bad," he said. "But we'll manage."

The sound of the rushing water shut out the rest of the world as he brushed his fingertips across her shoulders then ran them downward along her arms. She kept her eyes locked in his, still uncertain.

But what they were doing, what they were about to do, felt so familiar, so comfortable, that it was as if she was performing a dance she'd performed hundreds of times before. Her mind seemed to have shut down, at least the part that kept her safe.

Instead, another part seemed to be whispering, *It's okay. It's different now. Greg is different.*

So she didn't back away when he reached behind and easily found the clasp of her bathing suit top. In a quick, smooth motion, he unfastened it. His fingertips returned to her shoulders as he pulled down the narrow straps. She hunched forward, just enough that her bathing suit top dropped to the floor.

Greg's sharp intake of breath sounded like a gasp. Her self-consciousness deepened as she felt her nipples harden. Despite this scenario's familiarity, there was a feeling of newness about what they were doing, and she felt surprisingly shy.

Besides, she still wasn't convinced she was doing the right thing.

But it was too late. He was already pulling her close to him, crushing her breasts against his chest. She welcomed the warmth of his body, but it only took a moment before that feeling was replaced by another one entirely: a yearning that up until this point she'd been struggling to keep at bay.

Gently he lifted her face to his, leaning into a deep kiss. She caught her breath as he lightly touched his lips to hers before thrusting his tongue forward. Their mouths were still locked together as he ran the palms of his hands along her torso, down to her hips.

She didn't resist when he pushed down the sides of her bathing suit bottom. Instead, she stepped backward, just far enough to climb out of them. He pulled her close again, this time by cupping her buttocks. She could feel how hard he'd become, and she pressed her groin against his.

She was surprised when he suddenly stepped away.

"Hey, I'd better turn off the water or we're gonna have a flood," he said.

He leaned over the tub and turned off both handles with a swift jerking motion. The room was suddenly silent. He took her hand and bowed down in mock gallantry, motioning for her to get in.

She stepped over the edge of the tub, into the water. It was too hot, but she didn't protest. Instead, she climbed in, dropping down so the water covered her up to her shoulders.

"You're next," she said, looking up at him.

"I thought you'd never ask." He pulled off his underwear, sliding them easily over his thighs and letting them drop onto the floor, next to her crumpled bathing suit. Embarrassed, she averted her gaze.

He didn't seem to notice.

"Am I gonna fit in here?" he joked, climbing in.

Before she could answer, he moaned. "Oooh, that's hot!"

"You'll get used to it," she assured him.

She pressed her hips and thighs against the side of the tub to make room for him. He lowered himself onto his haunches, facing her, then kicked out his legs. He leaned back, resting his head against the opposite wall.

"Heaven," he declared. "I gotta get myself one of these housesitting gigs." Moving his eyebrows up and down comically, he added, "But in the meantime, we can enjoy yours."

He looked around for the start button, finding it behind his left shoulder.

"Ready?" he asked, his hand poised in mid-air.

She nodded. "Go for it."

He pressed down, and instantly they were surrounded by violently churning water. The motor made a rumbling sound so loud they had to yell to be heard.

"Awesome!" Greg exclaimed. "There's a water jet right behind my back."

"Me, too," Megan said.

"Y'know, I could get used to this."

This time, she didn't say anything, not sure if he was only talking about the bathtub.

And then, his clear blue eyes shining, he leaned forward with his hands submerged. Megan jumped when she felt his palms sliding against her thighs. He pulled her closer, her buttocks sliding easily over the wet surface of the tub. He moved closer, too, placing her legs on top of his, spreading them apart so that her feet were on either side of him.

"Close your eyes," he commanded.

As soon as she did, she felt his hands moving higher and higher along her thighs. Even though steam rose from the turbulent water, creating a mist as thick as fog, she shuddered.

And then his hand stopped, resting between her legs. His fingers sought out the familiar place, then began to stroke her in a light, rhythmic motion. At first, something inside her resisted. But as he continued caressing her, she gave in, letting the tension build.

"Oh-h-h," she murmured. "Don't stop."

Her breaths became gasps until the final release, the dissolution of the tightness into a series of delicious spasms. Her eyes flew open. She saw Greg's face in front of her, his eyes bright and his expression triumphant.

"Nice," he said. "What do you say we dry off and get in bed?"

She nodded. She felt as limp as a rag doll as he turned off the water jets then stood, reaching for her hand and pulling her up.

Yet she was on edge again as soon as they re-entered the bedroom. Not sure it was only because of Greg but unable to explain what else could have been the cause.

They crossed the room in silence then slid between the sheets. They were silky and cool, a welcome contrast to the steaming hot water.

Greg reached between her legs again, but she pushed his hand away.

"Too much," she insisted, whispering. "I'm still too sensitive."

Before she could protest, he was sliding toward the foot of the bed, pushing away the sheet. And then she felt his tongue, easily finding the right spot. Probing it gently, rhythmically . . .

Suddenly her eyes snapped open. Instinctively she jerked her head toward the doorway. She couldn't explain it, but she'd suddenly gotten the horrifying feeling someone was watching her.

But of course she saw nothing but an empty doorway.

You *are* tense, she thought. You're even starting to imagine things. Or maybe you're so ambivalent that you're looking for an excuse to stop.

Greg seemed to sense her reluctance.

"*Relax*, baby," he whispered in her ear.

She forced herself to close her eyes. To focus on what she felt instead of what she thought. Once again the tension grew as if something inside her was being pulled tighter and tighter. Finally, the sweet release. She heard herself moaning, marveling over how easy it was to let go.

To trust him again.

He slid back up so they were face-to-face, positioning himself over her and immediately pushing into her. Usually, she closed her eyes, wanting to concentrate on the physical sensations. But tonight she studied his face. His eyes were shut tight, his muscles were tensed, his mouth was twisted into what looked like an expression of pain.

He moved with more and more force, making the bed creak, until he finally let out a loud groan. A few seconds later he collapsed against her, his chest and thighs coated in sticky sweat.

"Wow," he said breathlessly, then laughed.

"My sentiments exactly," she replied.

He was silent for a few moments, catching his breath.

"It's okay if I stay overnight, isn't it?" he finally said, his mouth next to her ear on the pillow.

"Why wouldn't it be?" she asked, surprised.

"It's not really your house," he said, shrugging his left shoulder. "You're just borrowing it."

"It's fine," she assured him. "The owner is far, far away. He has no idea what's going on here."

And neither do I, she thought as almost immediately Greg's breathing became low and even, the sound eventually lulling her to sleep.

CHAPTER 21

H
e sits on the cold, hard basement floor, his body stiff, his hands clenched into fists, his heart pounding. Feeling the rage build inside him as he listens to the sounds above his head.

They're right above him. The two of them in the master bedroom, having just come inside from the pool.

"I'm all wet," he hears the intruder say. "Sorry about that."

As usual, she's accommodating. *Too* accommodating, assuring him that it's okay that he's dripping water all over the carpets, the bedspread.

He tenses even more when he hears him say, "Hey, you're freezing! Come over here. I'll warm you up."

Confident, just like always. Certain he'll get whatever he wants.

He is relieved by her reluctance. She mumbles something he can't hear, but he can guess what she's saying.

"C'mon, Megs," he wheedles. "It's me."

This guy is clearly someone who knows how to manipulate her. Who's in the *habit* of manipulating her.

Acting seductive. As if he's sure she can't help falling prey to his charms.

He bristles at the silence that follows. Frustrated that he has no way of knowing what's going on.

More talking, too soft for him to make out the words.

And then he jumps, startled by the sudden sound of water rushing through the pipes above his head. It's got to be the tub. She must have turned on the faucets. But why would she be taking a bath *now*, while he's still here?

The most obvious explanation fills him with horror.

But he already knows it's exactly what's happening. From the floor above, he can hear voices. Just as he feared, they're both in the bathroom. *Together.*

His heart pounds violently as he agonizes over what to do. Yet he already knows what he'll do. Even though he swore this was one risk he'd never take, he can no longer resist.

They won't even know, he tells himself. The rushing water will drown out any noise I might make. Besides, it's not as if they'll be focused on anything but themselves.

Slowly, silently, he begins climbing the stairs. Grasping the handrail, trying to minimize the impact of his weight. One step. Two steps.

Up above, the sound of turbulent water stops abruptly. At the same moment, the wood beneath his feet creaks.

He freezes, terrified that they've heard him. He stands perfectly still, his heart pounding, his skin coated in sticky sweat.

Waiting. Afraid he's about to be found out.

And then the house abruptly reverberates with the deafening thrum of the tub's motor, the violent rushing of water through the jets. The unexpected burst of noise nearly causes him to lose his balance.

But he exhales sharply. *Safe.*

Gently he places his hand on the doorknob and turns it as slowly as he can. Flinches as metal clicks against metal.

Yet he's certain they still have no idea he's so close.

As he pushes open the door, he hears the two of them in the bathroom, yelling to each other. He can picture them perfectly. Naked, in the tub.

The image sends a chill through him.

The way they're talking aggravates him even further. So casual, so completely uninhibited.

So *free.*

"There's a water jet right behind my back," the intruder yells.

"Me, too," Megan replies.

"Y'know, I could get used to this."

Anger rises up inside him at the notion that this interloper is starting to feel at home.

The silence that follows angers him even more.

Stealthily, quietly, he creeps through the hallway, toward the master bedroom. When he peers through the doorway, he sees they've left the bathroom door open.

"Close your eyes," he hears the intruder tell her.

His heart pounding, he makes his way through the bedroom, edging closer and closer toward the bathroom. Gently placing one foot in the front of the other on the thick carpeting, careful not to make a sound.

Wishing desperately he could see inside.

The mirror over the sink is large, but it's positioned too high to reflect the bathtub. Besides, he remembers a lesson he learned in a science class: if you can see someone's reflection in a mirror, that means the person can also see you.

What he hears next makes him freeze.

Megan, moaning. Then: "Don't stop!"

She's breathing so loudly he can hear her over the rushing water—or is he just imagining it? But he's sure he hears her let out a cry.

No! he thinks, his head feeling as if it's about to explode. *That should be* me!

And then the intruder speaks: "What do you say we dry off and get in bed?"

Startled, he turns, heading out of the bedroom. His footsteps are heavier than before, but he knows they won't notice.

They're too wrapped up in themselves.

He'd intended to make his way back downstairs. But as soon as he steps into the hallway, he stops. He can't bring himself to leave. Instead, he stands perfectly still, his back pressed against the wall next to the doorway, listening to the blood rushing through his temples.

From inside the bedroom, he hears soft footsteps on the carpet, the rustling of sheets, the creaking of the bed. He can picture the scene in his head.

It's not enough.

I want to watch. I have to see.

Moving in slow motion, he turns and peers through the bedroom doorway.

And instantly regrets it.

The image is chilling. Megan, *his Megan*, lying on the bed, the sheets pushed out of the way. Her eyes closed, her legs spread apart.

The intruder's head between them.

He steps away, struggling to keep a low moan from forcing its way out. He stuffs his fist into his mouth, the only way he can keep from crying out.

Even stronger is the impulse to rush into the room, to stop all this from happening.

He imagines grabbing the guy from behind, closing his hands around his throat, feeling the life drain out of him as he squeezes as tightly as he can, crushing skin and bone . . .

The scenario in his head is interrupted by more creaking of the bed, more of the grunts and cries and other horrific animal sounds.

Despite everything, he can't resist looking inside once again. When he involuntarily lets out a cry, neither of them seems to hear.

The guy is lying on top of her.

Pushing inside her. *Violating* her. *And she's letting him.* That simple fact cuts through him like a knife.

His head is swimming as he ducks back into the hallway. Lights flash before his eyes, and he places his hands over his ears as he tries to block out the sounds the two of them are making.

She hurt me, he thinks. Betrayed me in a way that will be hard to forgive.

And I have to let her know.

CHAPTER 22

Megan awakened with a start, her heart pounding and a sense of dread enveloping her even before she'd opened her eyes. The details of the night before flashed by like scenes from a movie. But that was no movie. That was real.

While her first reaction was regret, a feeling of hopefulness quickly pushed its way through. It was as if the morning sunshine had washed away all her apprehensions from the night before.

It's different this time, she told herself. This isn't the same old Greg. He's changed.

Still clinging to that thought, she wriggled across the sheets, expecting to snuggle against his warm body. Then realized she was alone. The feeling of intimacy that she'd expected would linger into the morning had vanished.

"Greg?" she croaked, her throat still coated with sleep.

"Hey!"

He appeared in the bathroom doorway, a towel wrapped around his naked torso. Grinning, he shook his head, sending a spray of droplets flying off his sopping wet hair.

"Nice shower," he announced. "I like that flowery gel stuff, too. It smells great. In fact, this whole place is totally awesome. You really lucked out."

"I know."

But she didn't want the two of them fifteen feet apart, talking about someone else's house. She wanted him in bed with her, his arm wrapped around her as she lay with her head on his shoulder, her thigh flung across his. Or maybe making love again.

She propped herself up on one arm, but kept the sheet pulled up modestly.

"Are you hungry?" she asked. "I could make brunch in that huge, wonderful kitchen."

"I have a better idea," he said, bending over to grab his shirt off the floor. "It's such a great day. Instead of staying cooped up inside, let's go out."

"Sure. What have you got in mind?"

"I was thinking we could drive to the beach. Venice, or maybe Malibu. We can find a place where we can eat outside, then take a long walk on the sand. What do you think?"

"It sounds like fun," she said, already climbing out of bed.

Megan and Greg zipped along Highway 1 with the top down, the wind blowing her hair wildly and the music so loud there was no point in even trying to make conversation.

After meandering along the coastline for a mile or two, they spotted the exact type of eatery she'd pictured. The roadside diner looked like a movie set, a one-story shack with weathered shingles and a red neon sign flashing, "OP N." It struck her as nothing short of miraculous that it had managed to stay in business even as multi-million dollar mansions sprang up all around it.

Despite the fact that it was surprisingly crowded, they scored a table outdoors, on the deck. The view of the Pacific was spectacular, with drops of sunlight dancing on the waves like frolicking fairies. Their waitress chewed gum and wore a pink uniform, their coffee cups were never empty, and the stack of blueberry pancakes she ordered was comically high.

She knew she should feel as if she was living in a storybook moment. But something was missing. Just as she'd noticed when she woke up, there was no sign of the intimacy of the night before. No feeling of connection. Instead, Greg chattered away. Filling her in on even the most minute details of his life, as if he just assumed she'd be interested.

"It's funny," he said, plunging his fork through his omelet. "Lately I've had this craving to watch classic movies. Like last week I rented this classic horror film about zombies. It's called *Night of the Living Dead*. Ever hear of it?" Before she even had a chance to answer, he launched into a monologue about the movie.

After brunch, they drove to Venice and poked around the shops. Then they took the long stroll on the beach he'd promised. She waited for him to take her hand, or even sling his arm around her. Instead, he seemed stiff. Distant, somehow.

"So here's the thing," Greg finally said, gazing out ahead instead of looking at her. "You know that new business venture I told you about? U-Tube?"

"What about it?"

"I'm gonna need some seed money. Y'know, funds to get me started. There's going to be a lot of start-up costs. Hiring people, advertising, even basic stuff like incorporating. It all costs money."

Megan frowned. "But I thought you said something about having a business partner."

"I do! And he's totally committed! In fact, he's investing ten thousand dollars of his own money, right up front."

"Okay," she said hesitantly. "So what's the problem?"

Greg took a breath, so deep it was practically a sigh. "He expects me to match it. Y'know, since we're going into this as equal partners."

This time, Megan was silent.

"Anyway, I know you're one of those people who's really on top of handling their money," he went on, his eyes still not meeting hers. "And I thought maybe you'd be able to help me out. Not with the whole ten grand, necessarily, but—"

"So that's what all this is about?" she cried, coming to a halt. "You want me to give you money?"

"*Lend* it!" Greg protested. "I'll get it all back to you, with interest! As soon as this thing takes off, which I'm absolutely certain is gonna happen—"

"Take me home," Megan insisted. "Now!"

"Hey! Megs!" Greg's tone had gone from confident to pleading.

"I mean it, Greg." Tears stung her eyes as she added, "I knew this was a mistake. I don't know what I was thinking."

You should have known better, she berated herself as she stalked off, the fine sand sucking her down and making it hard to walk quickly. How could you have been naïve enough to let yourself get *used* like this? Especially by Greg, who you know so well.

Back in his car, it quickly became apparent that they'd be traveling in silence. The only sound was the radio, turned up even louder than before.

It was dark by the time they pulled up in front of the house. Megan scrambled out of the car, as if she couldn't get away fast enough. But after a moment's hesitation, she turned back.

"Do me a favor?" she asked.

"Of course, Megs," Greg said, looking up at her with puppy dog eyes. "Anything."

"Don't call me again. *Ever!*"

She turned and marched up the driveway, blinking to stop her eyes from stinging. She glanced over her shoulder just long enough to watch his car disappear down Sierra Avenue.

"What an idiot," she muttered. But it was herself she was labeling, not Greg.

She'd already decided that even though the air was cool, she was heading straight for the pool, the only antidote she could think of.

She was still fuming as she neared the front door, key in hand. But she stopped in her tracks. She was positive she'd left the living room light on. She'd done nothing about fixing the broken porch light, and she'd had a feeling she might not get home until after nightfall. Yet the front room was dark.

Maybe the bulb burned out, she thought.

She unlocked the door, trying to brush away her uneasiness. First thing, she reached for the light switch next to the front door and flicked it on.

Then let out a shriek.

CHAPTER 23

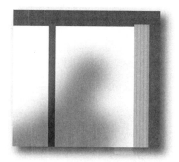

O h, my *God!*" she cried. She stood in the doorway, her mouth open and her hand, still clasping the key, frozen in mid-air. All around her was chaos. Every one of the pillows had been strewn around the room—not just the throw pillows, but even the couch cushions, all six of them pulled off the frame. The lamps were lying on their sides, the bulb in one of them smashed to bits. Her books and CDs littered the carpet, along with all the decorative items that had previously been displayed on the wall unit.

"What *happened?*" she moaned. And then: "Who could have done this?"

She suddenly remembered she wasn't the only one who lived here.

"Endora?" she called.

Picking her way through the wreckage, she headed toward the kitchen. "Endora, where are you? Are you here? Are you okay?"

The cat met her halfway, in the dining room. Megan scooped her into her arms and buried her face in her soft fur.

"My God, Endora!" she whispered. "What happened? Tell me!"

Endora meowed loudly. Megan almost believed she was trying to tell her what she saw.

"At least you're all right," she said.

Endora meowed again then wriggled out of her grasp. She leaped to the floor, then gazed up at Megan imploringly.

She realized that even with all that had happened, the cat was still hungry.

To further prove her point, Endora led her into the kitchen. Megan followed reluctantly, afraid of what she might find.

Even though she'd tried to brace herself for the worst, she let out another cry when she saw that the kitchen was in the same state as the living room. All the pots and pans had been pulled out of the cabinets and dumped on the floor.

A drawer of dishtowels and potholders had also been emptied out, along with the silverware drawer. Knives and forks and spoons were strewn around the room, mixed together with can openers and whisks and all the other gadgets that were once neatly stored.

Some of the plates and bowls had joined them, a few broken but most still intact. The exception was the wine glasses that, for her at least, doubled as champagne glasses. Every single one had been smashed.

But what was worse was the food.

The refrigerator had been completely emptied out. And its contents hadn't just been shoved onto the floor. From the looks of things, they were thrown.

A chunk of cheese, still wrapped in plastic, sat in a puddle of milk, with several pieces of fruit and a stick of butter. Three or four cartons of yogurt had opened, the force of being smashed against the floor sending globs of slippery, pastel-colored mush flying so that large splatters dotted the lower cabinets.

The sight of the destruction and chaos, all of it deliberate, made her dizzy. Megan found herself remembering all the other things that had happened in the house that had unsettled her, occurrences that had struck her as odd—at least until they'd turned out to have perfectly reasonable explanations.

She wondered if any of it meant anything.

But she quickly pushed that thought aside, finding the notion simply too overwhelming to deal with. She retrieved Endora's bag of food, which appeared to be untouched.

Her hands shook as she poured the usual amount into her bowl.

She left the cat to eat, then took a deep breath and continued her tour of the house. She went into her bedroom, once again trying to prepare herself. In fact, when she flicked on the overhead light and saw that all her clothes had been tossed on the bed and the floor, she wasn't surprised. She picked her way through the shoes and sunglasses lying on the carpet, to the bathroom.

She thought that by this point she'd grown accustomed to the dishevelment. But when she walked into the bathroom, she burst into tears.

There was something disturbing about seeing all her cosmetics and lotions and shampoo poured onto the floor, the empty bottles lying next to the mishmash of colors and textures. Even her expensive shower gel had been thrown into the mix.

Whoever did this had even taken the time to empty out her toothpaste, squeezing what was left of the tube over the mess glommed onto the tile floor.

She grabbed a few sheets of toilet paper and used them to wipe her eyes. Then backtracked through the bedroom to survey the rest of the house.

Fortunately, the lock on John's office appeared to be intact. There were other areas that also appeared untouched, including the sheets and towels stacked up in the linen closet.

Maybe whoever did this thought they heard someone coming, she thought. Maybe they heard me coming.

Her feelings of horror and despair were instantly replaced by fear.

What if they're still in the house?

The thought that she should simply get out occurred to her. But having been through the entire house without seeing any signs that anyone was still here quashed that idea. Besides, it was Sunday night and she was tired and she had nowhere else to go.

So she pulled out her cell phone and called 9-1-1.

While she waited for the police to show up, Megan was careful not to touch anything. As tempting as it was to put things back in order—to toss her shoes back into the closet and mop up the milk—she left things exactly the way she'd found them.

Even though she was expecting the police, *waiting* for them, she jumped when just a few minutes later she heard a loud knock at the door. She dashed over and flung it open.

But instead of finding a police officer, she was standing face-to-face with Russell. He was wearing a black sweatshirt, the hood pulled up over his head. He was doing that blinking thing, over and over again.

"Are you okay, Megan?" he asked anxiously. His eyes shifted over her shoulder, as if he was trying to get a look inside the house.

Rather than being grateful, she was instantly on the defensive.

"What do you mean, am I okay?" she demanded. "Why wouldn't I be?"

He stepped back slightly, as if he was startled. "I—I thought I heard somebody scream," he stuttered. "It sounded like you."

"This isn't a good time, Russell," she said, her tone sharp.

"Because if you've got a problem," he went on, "I might be able to help. In fact, I'd *like* to help."

"Listen to me, Russell," Megan said, her last traces of patience fading fast. "I want you to stop hanging around me so much. I know you think you're being nice, leaving me flowers and all that—"

"Flowers?" he repeated, blinking.

"Look, I can't deal with you!" she snapped. "Not now, not ever! I want you to stop bothering me. Don't talk to me, don't stand in the driveway, don't even *look* at me! In fact, if I see you anywhere near the house again, I'm going to call the police. Just leave me alone!"

He opened his mouth again, but she slammed the door before he had a chance to speak.

When she heard another loud knock, she peered through the front window before opening the door. This time, she wanted to make sure the person standing on the other side of the door was wearing a police uniform.

"Officer Garcia, Pasadena Police. Are you Ms. Quinn?" asked the cop. He was short, about her height, with black hair and dark brown eyes. "The person who reported a break-in?"

She nodded, then stepped aside to let him in.

She studied him as he surveyed the living room, expecting his face to register horror, or at least dismay.

Instead, he said, "I've seen worse. So tell me what happened."

He'd already pulled out a spiral notepad. She told him the basics: what time she left the house, what time she returned, that she hadn't touched anything.

"Anything taken?" Officer Garcia asked.

"Not that I know of. Nothing of mine, anyway."

She responded to the cop's puzzled expression by explaining, "I don't really live here. I'm just the housesitter. In fact, I haven't even told the owner about this yet."

"So you don't actually know if anything that belongs to the homeowner is missing."

She shook her head. "But he's got most of his important stuff locked up in one room. As far as I can tell, whoever did this didn't get in there."

"I'll check it out," the cop said. "The rest of the place, too."

He started with the front door, rattling the knob, studying the metal plate around the lock.

"It doesn't look like anybody tampered with this lock," he reported.

She followed him as he moved on to the rest of the house, occasionally jotting something down on his pad of paper. He checked the back door and the windows, then took even more time with the locked door.

"What'd you say is in here?" he asked.

"I'm not exactly sure," she replied. "Like I said, the owner told me it's all his important stuff. Papers and computers, I guess. He works from home."

"The lock looks untouched," he commented. "Whatever he's got in there should be fine."

At the end of his tour, he turned to her and said, "I'm not finding any signs of a break-in. But what about those glass doors in the bedroom that lead outside to the pool? I noticed they're unlocked. Did you leave them that way?"

She was startled by his question, but thought for a moment. "I suppose it's *possible . . .*"

The cop shot her an I-told-you-so look.

"I have a feeling that's how they got in," he said. "Believe me, you're not alone. People forget to lock those fancy French doors all the time."

The French doors? Megan thought woefully. And here I've been so conscientious about making sure the *back* door was locked!

The cop ran his eyes over her fleetingly then asked, "You got a boyfriend? Or an ex-boyfriend? Somebody who might be mad at you?"

"I was out with my boyfriend when this happened," she replied, not wanting to explain her relationship with Greg in any more detail. "I'm his alibi."

"How about somebody else, somebody from your past? It could even be a female."

Again, she shook her head. This was an exercise she'd already performed: running through a list of everyone she knew in L.A.

"Hardly anybody even knows where I am," she said. "I just started housesitting here a week ago."

"So it was most likely the homeowner who was the target."

"I guess." She thought for a few seconds, then asked, "Is it possible this was just a random thing? Like maybe some teenagers who thought it would be fun to come into somebody's house and mess up their stuff? Or drug addicts? Or people who are just plain crazy?"

"Not likely," the cop said. "Even Charles Manson, who's my favorite example of 'just plain crazy,' picked out somebody in advance."

She shivered. "But that was different, right? There aren't many people in the world who would do something like that, are there?"

She searched the police officer's face, looking for reassurance. Instead, he said, "I'd advise you to keep your doors and windows locked twenty-four/seven. Whenever you leave the house, especially at night, keep your wits about you. Just check around to make sure nobody's out there who's not supposed to be.

"And keep thinking about who you know who might have done this." Looking around one more time, he added, "It looks to me like this was done by somebody who was familiar with the place."

Megan just nodded.

"In the meantime," he said, "you'd better let the owner know what happened."

The cop was heading for the front door when Megan cried, "Wait!"

He turned back. "Did you remember something else?"

"Not exactly." She bit her lip, wondering how, exactly, to explain. "I wanted to mention that I've noticed some strange things going on around here."

"Really." The cop's eyes narrowed. "Like what?"

She hesitated, thinking of all the unusual things that had happened over the past week. The broken porch light and the glass that held Greg's flowers both being shattered the same night, Endora getting locked up in the linen closet, John's shirt being straightened up in the drawer, even little things like her favorite lipstick vanishing.

Then there was the strange feeling she'd gotten the night before, the feeling she was being watched, that someone else was in the house . . .

But she had nothing concrete, nothing other than feelings and impressions and coincidences to tell him about. So she shook her head and said, "Never mind. I'm just spooked because of what happened here."

For the first time, the cop smiled. "Hey, it could happen to anybody. Of course you're upset. Just keep the doors and windows locked, like I said. And if you have somebody who could come stay with you—girlfriend, boyfriend—it might not be a bad idea to give them a call."

"Right. Thanks."

"And don't wait to let the homeowner know about this." Shaking his head, he added, "Poor guy isn't gonna be happy."

She closed the door after him then immediately turned the lock, just as he instructed.

Just as she always did.

Am I losing my mind? Megan wondered, staring with disbelief at the chaos all around her—a chaos that, as sickening as it was, was hers to deal with. *Did I really leave the French doors unlocked?*

She decided she must have. There was no other logical explanation.

Unless whoever did this had a key. A friend of John's, an angry ex-girlfriend of his, even those sneaky cleaning people who had a way of slipping in and out whenever they pleased. Megan suddenly felt completely weighed down by the fact that she might never know who was responsible.

She glanced around again, this time with a more objective eye. She realized that cleaning all this up was going to take some effort. But first, there was an even more onerous job looming ahead of her: calling John in Minnesota and telling him what happened.

CHAPTER 24

Megan was filled with dread as she retrieved her cell phone from her pocketbook and sank onto the couch. She punched the right keys and was dismayed that John picked right up.

"Hey, Megan," he greeted her, as usual sounding cheerful. "How's life in Pasadena?"

"Not so great," she replied. "Something happened."

She could feel the mood shift at his end.

"That doesn't sound good," he said somberly. "Is there a problem with the house?"

"I'm afraid so." She took a deep breath. "I went out for the day, and when I came home, somebody had come in and—"

She stopped herself from saying "trashed the place," figuring that description was too strong. Not that it wasn't accurate, just that she didn't see any reason to alarm him any more than necessary.

"Someone messed up some things in the house," she said instead. "But it was mostly my stuff. I mean, nothing of yours was broken. At least nothing of value. Just some dishes and glasses and—"

"Wait a second," he interrupted. "You're telling me that someone broke into my house?"

"I'm afraid so."

"Are you all right?" he demanded. "You weren't hurt, were you?"

"I'm fine," she assured him.

"Did you call the police?"

"That's the first thing I did," she replied. "A cop came over and filed a report. But frankly, it didn't seem like catching whoever did this was much of a priority."

She hesitated before admitting, "He did say it was possible I'd left the French doors in the bedroom unlocked. But I really don't think I did. I'm always careful about that kind of thing. I'm super-responsible!"

She didn't give him a chance to respond. "I promise I'll clean everything up," she went on, speaking quickly. "And as far as I know, nothing was taken. And they didn't get into your home office. It turns out you're wise to keep it locked."

"That's all good news," John said. He took a deep breath. "And so is the fact that you're all right. That's the main thing. I'm so glad you weren't home when it happened."

Megan shuddered at the thought of someone else coming into the house while she was there.

"Look, John, I'm really sorry about this," she said. "I don't think it was my fault, but if you want me to move out, if you want to find somebody else to housesit—"

"Don't be silly!" John insisted. "Even if you did accidentally leave the doors unlocked, you had no way of knowing something like this might happen. As long as nothing was taken and none of my valuable stuff was damaged . . . In fact, this makes me even happier that you're there in the house to keep watch over it. The sad fact is that there are a lot of creeps out there."

Megan swallowed. "Actually," she said slowly, "the police officer said it was most likely somebody who knows you." Her voice thickened even more as she said, "Or someone who knows *me*. I told them that was practically impossible, though, that only a few of my closest friends know I'm here. And you, of course."

He sighed. "All this must have been such a shock. Are you sure you're holding up?"

She was slightly embarrassed by how concerned he was about her—especially since she'd assumed he'd be completely freaked out over his house being invaded. "Honestly, I'm fine. A little shaken up, as you can imagine, but otherwise I'm doing great. Endora is, too."

"That's such a relief," John said. "Look, don't worry about the broken wineglasses. They weren't expensive. Besides, things can be replaced."

"What matters," he concluded, "is that you and Endora are both okay. That's the only thing that's important."

After she and John hung up, Megan remained sitting on the couch, still clasping the phone in her hand. For the first time she could remember, the house seemed cold.

But something else didn't feel right. Something about their conversation. She immediately realized what it was.

"Don't worry about the broken wineglasses," John had said.

But she didn't recall saying that it was specifically wineglasses that got broken. The way she remembered it, all she'd said was glasses. But you can't be sure, she told herself. Besides, maybe you said *glasses* and he just assumed you meant *wineglasses*.

She decided that she was still so upset by the experience that she could hardly think straight, much less remember every single word she said on the phone or figure out what John was thinking.

She thought about the cop's suggestion that she call a friend to stay with her. That would probably be Elissa.

But Elissa had to get up early for work tomorrow. Besides, Megan was exhausted—too exhausted to go through the whole story all over again, then wait for her to come over. She'd also have to mention where she'd been all day and into the night. Including *who* she was with.

You'll be fine, she told herself, even though she wasn't feeling anything close to fine.

She cleaned up the bathroom then tackled the more demanding mess in the kitchen. Next she straightened up the rest of the house, putting the living room lamp back in place and stuffing her clothes back into the dresser drawers.

As she made her way down the hallway, toward the bedroom, she started to walk by John's locked office. Then stopped.

Who *is* he? she wondered. And why would someone want to break into his house and trash it? She hesitated for a moment, then tried the knob. It refused to turn in her hand. She ran her hand along the top of the frame, looking for a key. She was actually relieved when she didn't find one.

But instead of continuing on to the bedroom, she went back into the kitchen. When she found Endora stretched out near her water bowl, she scooped her up into her arms. For the first time since she'd moved into the house, Megan brought the cat to bed, not wanting to sleep alone.

CHAPTER 25

Megan slept fitfully that night, never allowing herself to fully lose consciousness. She lay in bed with the blankets pulled up to her chin, staring into the darkness.

Watching. Listening. Worried that this unsettling episode wasn't over.

The few times she did manage to drift off, she jerked awake at the slightest sound: the refrigerator whirring, a plane overhead buzzing, Endora's water bowl scraping against the tile floor.

The sun had already begun to lighten the sky by the time she fell into a deep sleep, exhausted by the ordeal. Yet even in her dreams, she was unable to let go of the horror of walking in the front door, replaying the same scene again and again. The images in her head seemed so real that she was surprised when Endora's impatient meowing awakened her.

She dragged herself out of bed. Endora trotted after her, still complaining.

"You poor kitty cat," Megan said as the two of them headed for the kitchen. "I bet you're upset, too. After all, you're the one who witnessed the whole horrible thing."

She glanced down at the mass of orange fluff beside her and sighed. "I sure wish you could tell me who did this."

She put together a makeshift breakfast. First she rifled through the cabinets until she found a box of crackers that had remained unscathed. Then she put a cup of water for tea into the microwave, perching on a stool while she waited for it to boil.

Even though the sun was shining brightly, she was still on edge. She'd never experienced a violation like this before.

Someone intruding on what was supposed to be her little piece of the planet, her own personal haven where she was safe from whatever the rest of the world might inflict on her . . . It reminded her of the way she'd felt after experiencing her first substantial earthquake, not long after she moved to L.A.

Then, like now, she'd felt betrayed. As if something she'd just assumed all her life was stable, a given she could always count on, suddenly turned out to be completely different from what she'd believed unquestioningly to be true.

At least as disturbing was the fact that she had no idea of the intruder's agenda.

As she sat with Endora curled up in her lap, sipping her cup of tea, she found herself thinking about John again, and how little she actually knew about him.

I was so busy making him trust me *that it never occurred to me to think about whether he was somebody* I *could trust. But someone he knows is obviously angry enough to break in and trash his house.*

When the doorbell rang, she jumped.

Her first thought was that it was Greg. But when she dashed into the living room and peeked out the front window, she didn't see his car. Instead, she was surprised to see the same white car that had shown up a few days earlier. Jacob Maarse Florists.

She opened the door and found the same pimply teenager standing on the doorstep.

"Hey, I remember you!" he said cheerfully.

He handed her a long white box, identical to the last one, adding, "You sure are popular!"

She was too confused by what was happening to reply.

From John? she thought, fumbling for a tip. *Again?*

As she closed the front door, she told herself she should be glad he didn't blame her for his house being trashed. But instead, she was annoyed.

It's too much, she thought, feeling slightly dazed as she walked into the kitchen with the box. *The flowers, the champagne, the phone calls . . . Our deal was that the house was mine to enjoy, not that he'd act as if he still lived here and I was his roommate.*

Or his live-in girlfriend.

She dropped the box on the counter and took off the lid. She wasn't at all surprised that a dozen perfect yellow roses were lying inside.

Even though she dreaded reading the card, she rustled through the green tissue paper until she found it.

"Sorry you had to deal with a break-in," it read. "Wish I was there to comfort you and help you get through it."

"Ugh," she said aloud.

Why does he keep doing this? she thought. Why can't he just leave me in peace?

He's only trying to be nice, she told herself, feeling a little bit guilty. He obviously knows how traumatic this was for me. Maybe he even feels partially responsible. After all, this is his house.

Yet despite her rationalizations, her impatience over his intrusiveness overrode her attempts at feeling grateful. She didn't even feel like putting the roses in water.

Telling herself that the water-filled plastic tips would keep them safe, she left them on the counter, next to the box. She headed to the bedroom and pulled on the same pants and shirt she'd worn the day before. As she slid into her sandals, she grabbed her car keys and made a beeline for the door.

Suddenly, she couldn't wait to get out of there.

Megan tried to force herself out of her bad mood by focusing on being efficient. She filled her car with gas, bought a pound of ground coffee at Peet's, and replaced most of her makeup and the other personal items that had been destroyed at the drug store. Her last stop was Trader Joe's, where she restocked her supply of yogurt and gingersnaps and a few other staples. By the time she pulled into the driveway, she'd calmed down. The vandalism episode was over. It was something she'd managed to get through.

As for John's insistence on sending her flowers, she decided that it was about him—that it actually had very little to do with her.

Clutching her bundles, she headed up the driveway, already planning the rest of her day. She decided she'd spend it sitting by the pool, writing. At least, after she put a little more time in on her résumé.

And after she took a swim, she thought as she unlocked the front door.

She sailed into the kitchen, already looking forward to getting into the pool. As soon as she reached the doorway, she froze. Staring, trying to digest what she was looking at: the second bouquet of roses, carefully arranged in a vase on the counter.

CHAPTER 26

Megan dropped her packages onto the counter, grabbed her cell phone, and punched in John's number. "Hey, it's you!" he greeted her cheerfully. "How's everything going?"

"As a matter of fact," she replied, "that's why I'm calling. Something really strange just happened."

"You sound upset."

"I am." She paused to take a breath. "I got the flowers you sent this morning."

"I hope you liked them."

"They're beautiful," she said, her voice flat. "The thing is, I didn't have time to put them in water before I ran out to do a couple of errands. But when I came home, they were in a vase." She swallowed, then added, "Which means somebody came into the house."

John exhaled deeply. "That would be Tom."

"Tom?" she repeated. "Who's Tom?"

"A friend of mine."

"I don't understand."

He sighed. "This is kind of . . . awkward. Tom is someone I asked to stop by from time to time, just to check on the place."

Anger rose inside her as she said, "You told this friend of yours it was okay to come into the house when I wasn't here?"

"I gave him a key before I left," John said. "I guess he figured he'd let himself in and take a look around to make sure everything was in order. After what happened yesterday, I mean."

"Wait a minute," she said, her irritation growing. "This friend of yours, a perfect stranger I've never even heard of, much less met, has your permission to come into the house where I'm living whenever he feels like it, just to look around?"

"I guess I never really thought it through," he said, sounding apologetic. "It didn't occur to me that you might consider it an imposition."

"It didn't—*what?*"

"I also didn't realize that was what Tom intended to do," he went on, speaking quickly. "I mean, before I left I asked him to keep an eye on things, and then I called him this morning to tell him about the break-in."

"So for some reason he just assumed he had your permission to waltz into the house whenever he felt like it?"

"Look, I'm sorry," he said. "It didn't occur to me that it would play out this way. I was just trying to make sure things were back to normal.

"Besides," he added, his tone light-hearted, "at least he got the flowers into water."

"I wasn't gone that long," she protested, then wondered how she'd ended up on the defensive. "If you don't trust me, why did you leave your house and Endora and all your possessions in my care?"

"I *do* trust you," he insisted. "And I'm sorry if you're upset. The last thing I want to do is upset you."

"Then please tell this friend of yours not to simply come in whenever he feels like it."

"I understand completely, and I promise to do exactly that." Brightening, he said, "So have you been enjoying the house?"

"Yes," she said dully.

"And the pool? Are you still getting a lot of use out of it?"

"Yes. It's been on the cool side, but I don't mind."

"Well, I'm sure it's not as cold as it is here in Minneapolis," he said. "People here keep telling me I've got thin blood because I'm from California, but I don't see how anybody could be comfortable in temperatures like these."

"How cold is it?" she asked without much interest.

"Cold enough that I can see my breath in the morning," he said, sounding as if he was bragging. "I've never experienced that before."

"I'm sure you'll get used to it," she said, anxious to get off the phone. This episode had left a bad taste in her mouth, and she was finding it a strain to make chitchat with him. "I guess I should let you get back to work. I'm sure you've got a lot of other things you should be doing."

"Definitely. But I'm always happy to hear from you, Megan. It's very important to me that you're happy. Feel free to call me any time."

After she'd hung up the phone, she could still hear that last sentence, echoing through her head.

There's something so peculiar about him, she thought. It was a thought she'd had many times before, but this time it was accompanied by a knot in her stomach.

This whole situation is strange, she decided. Living here like this, in someone else's space. And now I find out that some guy, some friend of John's, is coming into the house without me knowing it, looking at my stuff, moving around in the space where I'm living.

She was still grappling with the sense of unease all this had created in her when the house phone rang. She wondered if it was John, calling her back.

Hoping it wasn't, she answered.

"May I speak to John Davis?" a pleasant female voice asked.

"He's not here right now, but I'd be happy to take a message," Megan replied.

"That'd be great," the woman said. "This is the Pasadena Animal Shelter, and I'm calling about the cat Mr. Davis adopted."

"Right," Megan said, grabbing a pen and a pad of paper. "Endora."

"I remember him saying that was what he was going to name her." From her voice, Megan could tell she was smiling. "A Maine coon, right? They're so smart— and they make such great companions. In a way, they're more like dogs than cats. Anyway, we always make a routine call ten days or so after an adoption. We just like to follow up and make sure everything is going well, see if the new owner has any questions or concerns."

"Ten days?" Megan repeated, her pen poised in mid-air.

"That's right. That's usually enough time for the animal and the owner to get to know each other."

Confusion clouded Megan's thoughts. "I don't understand. Are you saying that John Davis adopted Endora ten days ago?"

"Yes, on Monday, October 11th."

"October 11th of this year?" Megan demanded.

"Of course." The woman at the other end of the line was clearly growing impatient.

"Do you know what time—" She decided to try a different strategy. "What time do you open on Mondays?"

"The Adoption Center opens at noon," the woman replied, her voice now crisp. "Maybe I should call back when Mr. Davis is at home."

"But this is important."

A loud *click* told her the woman had hung up.

Megan's head was spinning as she stood up, the phone still in her hand.

John only got Endora last Monday, a week and a half ago, she thought, nearly overwhelmed by the sense of horror that surrounded her. Some time in the afternoon. Right after we met at Peet's to talk about me housesitting for him.

He acquired Endora right after he acquired me.

But why would he have lied about having a cat? she wondered, her mind racing. Why would he even have been looking for a housesitter in the first place if he didn't have a pet that needed care every day? Especially when he had this friend of his, Tom, to look in on the house from time to time?

She lowered herself onto one of the stools, since the act of standing up suddenly seemed to require too much strength.

A lot of people who don't have pets get a housesitter, she told herself, rubbing her forehead with two fingers. They're worried about someone breaking in or a pipe bursting or a million other things that could go wrong . . .

But why run out and get a cat? It's almost as if once we met and he found out how anxious I was to housesit, he wanted to be sure he had a reason to need a housesitter.

She allowed herself to think about all the little things she'd found so disturbing but had pushed out of her mind so many times. All of them with perfectly reasonable explanations, each one innocuous enough by itself, but taken together forming a disturbing pattern.

The flowers she'd left on the counter moving to a vase, the appearance of her favorite champagne in the refrigerator . . . It was a list she'd run through again and again.

But it wasn't only *what* happened, but *when* it happened. The roses arriving right after Greg came over with a bouquet of his own. The Moet materializing the day after she and Greg talked about him not being able to afford such expensive champagne.

Then there were the phone calls. Not only that they were so frequent, but also that they always seem to come right after something significant, something strange, had happened. Almost as if somehow he knew exactly what she was doing.

What she was thinking.

A sick feeling had come over her, as if she was finally being forced to deal with something that had been lurking at the back of her mind for a long time. Her head throbbing and her stomach in knots, she walked through the house. Looking at everything around her with new eyes, trying to see things differently, to notice details that had escaped her up until now.

She stopped in front of the door to the locked room. Tried the lock, found it immovable.

Wondered why she hadn't been more interested in what he had in there, the one room of the house that had always been off-limits to her.

Then realized there was another part of the house that she'd never bothered to explore.

CHAPTER 27

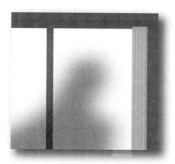

Megan's mouth was strangely dry as she walked over to another door. Asking herself why she'd never gone into the basement before. Immediately answering her own question: *because there was never any reason to.* All of a sudden, it seemed important to find out what was down there.

She reached for the knob, half-expecting it to be immovable. Instead, it turned easily. She wasn't sure whether she was glad or not.

Her hand trembled as she opened the door. When she was confronted by darkness, she hesitated.

It's a basement, she told herself. Of course it's dark down there.

She patted the wall, found a switch. A single naked bulb hanging from the ceiling went on, the light barely bright enough for her to see. She swallowed, then started down the wooden steps. Slowly, her heart pounding, afraid of what she might find but unwilling to go back.

"Anybody here?" she asked in a hoarse whisper.

The silence that followed was little consolation. She continued down the stairs, keeping an eye out for spiders.

Wishing that were her only concern.

"Hello?" she called when she reached the bottom, wanting to assure herself that no one was down here.

As if anyone who was hiding would answer.

No one is down here, she told herself, trying to calm her jackhammer heart.

She was reassured by the basement itself, which offered few hiding places. It was little more than a tiny room, a low-ceilinged concrete box that for some reason made her shudder.

Off to the right were concrete steps that led to the garden. She'd spotted the outer door while watering the flowerbeds but had no reason to do anything besides ignore it. Even in the dim light, she saw a flashlight on the top step, and she grabbed it.

The rest of the room was surprisingly bare, considering that there were few other storage areas in the house. She shined the flashlight around and saw that several cardboard cartons, sealed with duct tape, were stacked against one wall alongside a teak deck chair that had lost an arm. She also saw a few tools, a lantern, a plastic bucket, and a portable heater.

Ordinary stuff. The kind of things you'd find in anyone's basement.

Now that her curiosity had been satisfied, she was ready to go back upstairs. Still, she took one last look around the small room to assure herself that there was nothing here worth worrying about.

It was only then she noticed the stash underneath the stairs.

The space was dark enough that, from where she was standing, she couldn't make out the details of what was in the pile. She took a few steps closer and shined the flashlight on it. Thick fabric that looked like a blanket or a drop cloth, a few plastic jugs . . . the collection of items looked like more of the usual basement detritus.

Yet a flash of bright green that somehow didn't belong caught her eye.

She focused the flashlight's beam on the spot of green. It was the side of a cardboard box. Granola bars.

With her free hand, she pulled it out of the pile. And saw that it was half empty.

Running the flashlight over the entire stack, she took a closer look at what was stored there. The thick fabric was actually a sleeping bag that was folded up on top of a pillow. Most of the plastic jugs were filled with water. Only one was empty. When she examined it, she noticed that it smelled faintly of urine.

And then she saw a crushed coffee cup that was printed with the Peet's logo, lying on the floor. She picked it up, and a few drops of cold coffee spilled out.

She was started feeling sick. Dizzy, as if the room was spinning.

She dropped the paper cup and quickly put the flashlight back where she'd found it. She hurried up the stairs, nearly tripping when she'd almost reached the top.

She went into the kitchen, the brightest, airiest room in the house. As soon as she spotted Endora lying in a sunny spot, she scooped her up into her arms, craving comfort.

Oh, my God, she thought, sinking onto a stool and burying her face in the cat's soft orange fur. Does all that mean what I think it means—that someone's been down there?

Recently—even in the past week since I got here?

Or am I just being paranoid?

She replayed Elissa's teasing comment about John being a survivalist. It was true that there were plenty of people who kept stashes of food and water in their basements, and not all of them because they were afraid of the end of the world. An earthquake, a serious rainstorm, a terrorist attack . . . there was a whole list of good reasons to be prepared for the worst.

But the provisions she'd found in the basement wouldn't be enough for more than a day. Besides, there was that cup of coffee, left there recently enough that the few remaining drops hadn't yet dried up.

The scenario that had lodged itself in her head was something entirely different than someone wanting to be ready for the next big quake.

She considered calling the police. Then wondered what she'd tell them. She could picture Officer Garcia smiling sardonically as he explained that it wasn't illegal, or even suspicious, to store sleeping bags and bottled water in the basement.

Her thoughts were whirling so quickly that she couldn't manage to focus on any of them.

Am I crazy? she wondered. Am I taking normal occurrences that have perfectly good explanations and blowing them way out of proportion? Or is John someone other than the person he appears to be?

Questions kept buzzing around in her head. Snippets of conversation, too, things he said that at the time she barely paid attention to.

Things he told her about himself.

Like the company he worked for, which she'd never heard of. No one else seemed to have heard of it, either.

There are a million companies out there, she told herself. Maybe it's even his company, and he's a one-man operation but was trying to sound more important.

She suddenly wanted to find out.

She hopped off the stool, startling Endora. The cat leaped out of her arms, then jumped out of Megan's way as she dashed to her bedroom.

She grabbed her laptop off the dresser then took it back into the kitchen. At her approach, Endora skittered off, meowing with displeasure.

She deposited her computer on the island, waited impatiently while it booted up, then immediately logged onto the Internet.

When the Google page came up, she typed in "Kerwood Industries." She hit Return.

A question popped onto the screen: "Did you mean *Kirkwood* Industries?"

Megan frowned. *I could swear he said Kerwood,* she thought. Kirkwood was the name of a ski resort near Lake Tahoe, and she was certain she would have noticed the similarity.

She tried a different spelling. K-I-R-W-O-O-D. Google asked her the same question: "Did you mean *Kirkwood* Industries?"

She stared at the screen in confusion. *What am I missing?*

She started typing the word, "Kerwood" into the Google home page. Before she hit Enter Google suggested that she try "Kirwood Derby."

"Kirwood Derby?" she muttered. "What is that?" She tried it, just to see what came up.

A new set of listings appeared on the screen. Once again, she clicked Wikipedia, figuring it was the quickest, easiest way to get an idea of what the phrase meant. She was surprised when the biography of an actor named Durward Kirby came up. She skimmed it until she came across two sentences that she reread several times.

"Kirby's name was spoofed in the animated television series *The Rocky and Bullwinkle Show*, in which a man's derby-style hat was called the 'Kirward Derby'. The derby supposedly had magic powers that made its wearer the smartest person in the world."

Rocky and Bullwinkle. She'd heard of the show but didn't remember the details. She did a Google search, clicked some keys, and found herself back at Wikipedia. She learned that Rocky and Bullwinkle were the cartoon-character stars of two television shows that ran from 1959 through 1964.

Television sit-coms from the 1960s. Just like *Bewitched.* The show that was the source of "Endora," the name John chose for his cat.

Trying to ignore the wave of despair that was sweeping over her, Megan did a Google search for *Bewitched.* Just as she'd thought, the show ran from 1964 to 1972.

It could be a coincidence, she told herself. But even if it was, that didn't explain why there was no such company as Kerwood Industries.

Despite the fog in her brain, she suddenly had another thought. This one was more of a long shot. But her curiosity wouldn't allow her to let go of it.

"W—W—W—dot—w—e—a ..." she typed, then hit Enter.

A second or two later, the home page for weather.com appeared on the screen. At the top, in the blank space that said "Enter ZIP, City or Place (e.g. Disney World)," she began to type: M—I—N - N . . .

"Minneapolis, MN, USA" popped up before she completed the word. She swallowed hard, then clicked.

Almost immediately a new screen popped up. "68 degrees F," it read, with a cartoonish drawing of the sun.

She was startled. This wasn't what she'd expected.

She Googled "Minneapolis weather."

The first listing that came up was the website of a Minneapolis newspaper.

"We're having a heat wave!" the text read. "Instead of the down jackets Minneapolis residents usually wear this time of year, they're donning T-shirts and even sandals as temperatures hit record highs . . ."

Her heart thumped in her chest as, just to be sure, she checked the date of the posting. The date was today's.

Okay, she thought, swallowing hard, so he's not really in Minneapolis. But why is he pretending that he is? Instead of things becoming clearer, her brain was getting more and more muddled.

The ad, she thought. The "housesitter wanted" ad that got me here in the first place.

She Googled "Speedy's Pasadena" and the local area code, spotted a listing with the shop's phone number, grabbed her cell phone and dialed.

"Come on, come on," she muttered as it rang twice, three times, four times, then went to voice mail.

"Thank you for calling Speedy's Copy Shop. No one is available to take your call right now, but please leave a message and—"

"Idiot," Megan muttered as she hung up.

But she was already scrambling off the stool, tossing her phone into her purse and then rooting around for her car keys.

CHAPTER 28

Fifteen minutes later Megan sailed into Speedy's, out of breath even though she'd found a parking space right in front. She wasn't surprised that standing behind the counter was the same young man she'd spoken with the last time, the punk wannabe with the elaborate hairdo and the face decorated with metal.

"You're back," he said pleasantly. "Got that résumé ready to go?"

She suddenly felt as if she was wasting her time. The possibility that this store employee might be able to help her struck her as ridiculously remote.

Yet she was here.

"Actually, there's something else I wanted to ask you about," she told him. "A couple of weeks ago, I answered an ad someone had put up on your bulletin board." She pointed at the display of index cards and 8 ½ by 11 sheets of paper that formed a colorful collage near the entrance. "It was for a housesitting gig. I don't suppose you—"

"Sure, I remember that one," he said. "We don't get too many of those. Usually people use Craigslist or one of the housesitting websites that are out there. I figured maybe the guy didn't have a computer or something. Believe it or not, there are still people like that."

"I'm sure there are," she commented distractedly.

"And it wasn't that long ago that the guy finally came in and took it down," the clerk continued. "Maybe . . . early last week? I seem to remember him saying something about how he finally found the right person."

"This probably sounds crazy, but . . ." She hesitated, partly because her mouth had become so dry she had to swallow. "Do you have any sense of how long that ad was up there?"

The young man snorted. "I sure do. That thing was up there for ages."

Megan forced herself not to react. "You mean, like, days?"

"No-o-o. More like weeks. Maybe even months." He shrugged. "Our policy is not to remove anything that somebody's posted. We wait for whoever put it up to come take it down, and everybody's kind of on the honor system."

With a shrug, he added, "I figured this guy was the exception. That thing sat up there for so long that I figured he had to have found a housesitter back in the summer, when he first put it up, but then never bothered to come by again. I was pretty surprised that he finally showed up and took it down."

Megan's head was spinning so fast she felt weak.

Weeks, even months. Back in the summer.

Which meant John had spent a long time looking for someone to housesit for him.

The right person.

That was what he'd said, wasn't it? The first time they'd met, a week and a half earlier?

"With something this important, you want to make sure you've found the right person."

So it had all been a lie. Not only the name of his company, but also his story about finding out he was being sent out of town only the week before. All that business about how he'd been rushing to find a housesitter . . . he'd made it all up.

Just like he'd made up the fact that he had a cat. He hadn't adopted Endora until after they'd met. Which meant he'd set the whole thing up. He'd waited until he'd found the person he wanted to live in his house, then gone out and gotten a cat to make it look like he needed a housesitter.

And *she* was the one he'd chosen.

Even though she felt as if the room was spinning, Megan forced herself to replay what she could remember of their conversation the day they met. Tried to think of what she said that might have caused him to pick *her*.

She remembered almost all of what she'd told him about herself. That she was a single woman, pretty much alone in a strange new city with no place else to go. That she had no job. No family nearby. In other words, no ties. No place where she'd be missed. At least, not right away.

The right person.

Megan jumped when she suddenly heard the clerk say, "You look a little pale. Are you okay?"

She let out a high-pitched laugh. "I'm not sure."

She rushed out of the store, suddenly desperate for fresh air. Aside from feeling like she needed to breathe, she wasn't sure where she was going or what she'd do next.

But she was beginning to understand what had been happening. John had never left Pasadena. He'd been watching her while she'd been living in his house, keeping track of her comings and goings. Listening in on her conversations, too.

Which meant he'd been inside the house.

All the strange goings-on of the past week . . . every one of them had been John's doing.

She was suddenly nearly overcome with dizziness. Blindly she rushed over to her car, grabbing onto it to steady herself. Through the buzzing in her head, one thought stood out with perfect clarity: she had to get away from John's house.

The sooner, the better.

Megan's head was still buzzing and her stomach was in knots as she got into her car. Then instinctively locked all the doors.

She sat hunched over the steering wheel, covering her face with both hands. *I have to think. I have to figure out what to do.*

But she already knew what she was going to do. And she couldn't wait a moment longer. She grabbed her cell phone out of her purse, meanwhile forcing herself to take deep breaths. They were meant to relax her. But she wasn't having much success.

Calm down, she told herself. *You have to find a way to pull this off.*

She hit the keys on her cell phone that dialed his number. Her hands were trembling and her heart felt as if it was about to burst.

He answered on the second ring.

"Hey, Megan!" John said breezily. "Everything okay?"

"Everything's great," she replied, trying to sound as if she meant it.

"What's up, then?" he asked.

She noticed an unusual tightness in his voice. Wondered if she might simply be imagining it.

"Actually—" Her voice came out hoarse, and she coughed.

"Are you okay?" he asked.

"I'm fine. Something's stuck in my throat, that's all." This time, she took a deep breath before jumping in. "Actually, I called because there's something I have to tell you."

"Uh, oh," he said jokingly. "I don't like the sound of that."

Stay calm, she told herself. "I'm afraid I have to leave."

"Leave?" he repeated the word as if he didn't understand it.

"Leave Pasadena." Quickly she continued, "It's for a good reason, though. I got a new job, a really good one. But it means relocating."

"Where?" He asked.

She hesitated. She hadn't thought that far ahead.

"Sacramento," she said, blurting out the first place that came to mind.

He was silent for a few seconds. She hoped he couldn't hear her pounding heart through the phone.

"This is a new twist," he finally said. She was certain there was an edge to his voice, something she hadn't heard before.

"I know," she said, her voice meek. "Honestly, it just came up today."

"When are you thinking of going?"

"As soon as possible," she replied.

"But I'm still in Minneapolis," he said. "I haven't had time to make any arrangements."

"I could get one of my friends to come in and feed Endora," she offered. "Or maybe you could arrange for your friend Tom or the cleaning people to do it." She could hear her voice rising, the pitch higher than usual.

"You're the one I want," he insisted, his voice plaintive. And then, sounding gruff: "We had a deal."

"I know we did," she said. "And it wasn't a problem before. But now, well, everything's changed."

"I see." He was silent for a long time before he said, "Well, I guess there's really nothing I can do, is there? I mean, it's not as if I can force you to stay."

"I'm sorry things are working out this way," she said. "I didn't expect this to happen."

"Look," he said, "this is freaking me out a little. I just didn't see this coming. I'll need some time to think about what to do next. I'll call you back in a little while, okay?"

She was about to reply when she realized he'd already hung up.

CHAPTER 29

I have to get home, Megan thought. Then immediately corrected herself: *I have to get back to John's house.* She was driving along South Lake as fast as she dared when a light turned red and she was forced to stop. She muttered under her breath. But as she waited, she planned her strategy.

Mainly, how to move out as fast as she could.

Where to go, once she was out. Elissa's place probably, at least for a couple of nights. That was the most likely possibility. She decided to worry about that later. Right now, she had too many other things to think about.

She pounded the steering wheel lightly with her fist as she stared at the light, which stubbornly refused to turn green. Wondered if she should called Elissa at work and ask her to come to the house with her.

Then realized Elissa wasn't free to run out of her office any time she wanted to. Besides, the last thing she wanted to do was wait for her to show up.

I'll be in and out of there in a flash, she told herself. I'll just grab everything I can and throw it all into a suitcase.

But her main reason for going back was Endora.

I have to take her with me, she thought. I'm not about to leave her with someone like John. He obviously doesn't care about her at all. The only reason he adopted her in the first place was so he'd have a reason to need a housesitter.

The light finally turned green. Megan stepped on the gas and her car darted forward. She veered sharply around the car in front of her when it slowed down to make a left turn.

I have to get out of there. The words kept playing through her head like the proverbial broken record.

The same phrase still dominated her thoughts as she pulled into the driveway at 55 Sierra and jerked to a halt. She grabbed her purse and jumped out of the car, slamming the door behind her.

When she reached the front door, she hesitated. A sense of dread had come over her, the feeling that she didn't know what she'd find inside.

Maybe I should just leave. Just get back in my car and—

Endora, she thought. I have to get her out of there.

Besides, I'll be in and out in a flash. Five minutes. That's all I need.

She put her key in the lock and turned it. As she stepped inside, she scanned the living room, her ears pricked. But she heard nothing, saw nothing, out of the ordinary.

It was quiet. Absolutely silent, in fact.

Still, just to be safe, she wasted no time in packing up her stuff.

Her first stop was the master bedroom. As she hurried down the hallway, she realized that there really was no one here—including Endora. The cat usually came out of hiding as soon as she came in, padding over to greet her and make sure she got her share of stroking and ear scratching.

Today, there was no sign of her.

I'll find her after I pack, Megan decided.

She forced herself to focus on gathering up all her possessions. Once she left, there was no way she was coming back. She dropped her pocketbook onto the bed and turned to the closet. She pulled dresses and blouses off their hangers, two and three at a time, then tossed them onto the bed behind her.

She'd just dragged out the suitcase stored at the bottom when she heard a soft meow.

"Endora?" she called. "Where are you?"

She hurried into the hallway, following the sound. She didn't see her, but she kept calling her name. Her eyes traveled up and down the hall. And then she froze.

The door to the locked room was ajar.

Her heart began to pound furiously.

Who could possibly have unlocked it? she wondered.

The cleaning people, she thought. Or maybe Tom, the man with the keys, made another surprise visit.

Or maybe it was John.

Just get out, a voice inside her head commanded. *Forget about Endora and run.*

She heard it again: *Meow.*

There was no mistaking it. It was Endora, and her mewing sounded like a plea. The kind of noise made by an animal in trouble. It seemed to be coming from inside that room.

Megan hesitated. *I have to take her with me.*

She was still debating whether or not to go inside when she heard the cat one more time.

Meow.

Even before she was aware that she'd made a decision about what to do, Megan moved along the hallway, toward the open door. All around her was silence. Only the sound of her footsteps, the soft thud of the soles of her shoes on the carpet, cut into it.

That and the throbbing in her temples.

When she reached the door, she hesitated. Then heard Endora's desperate cry for help once again.

Her heart thumping loudly, she pushed the door so that it opened wider then peered through the opening.

Inside, she saw only darkness.

She blinked, gradually realizing that the blinds on the window were drawn so tightly that none of the brightness from outside could creep through the slats.

Still standing in the doorway, she reached inside. She slid her fingers along the wall, searching for a light switch. When she found it, she flipped it on. Light from a ceiling fixture filled the room.

She blinked, expecting to find a home office stocked with computers and file cabinets and desks. So she was surprised to discover that the mysterious locked room was just another bedroom.

A very nice bedroom, in fact, maybe even nicer than the master bedroom. In addition to a queen size bed flanked by two night tables and covered with a bright yellow bedspread scattered with throw pillows, there was a small sitting area with a loveseat and a low coffee table. The walls, also a cheerful shade of yellow, were dotted with artwork. A Hockney print of a swimming pool hung above the bed, while three black and white photos of Yosemite National Park were lined up side-by-side above the small couch.

In one corner there was a small kitchen set-up, comprised of a mini-fridge and a microwave on a rectangular table. Directly opposite, in the other corner, there was a bathroom. Through the open door, she could see the sink, surrounded by a granite counter. It reminded her of a nice hotel room.

Yet it wasn't nearly as sterile. The table tops, the closet, even the bathroom were outfitted with someone's possessions.

Now that the mystery had been solved, she realized that there was still no sign of Endora.

She stepped farther inside, mainly looking for the cat but also fascinated by how ordinary the room was. She wondered if the fact that it was just another bedroom was an indicator that she'd blown everything out of proportion.

She was also curious about who it belonged to. From the looks of things, a woman lived here. Or *had* lived here. A girlfriend, a sister, a mother, even a roommate.

Get out, a voice inside her head told her. *You shouldn't be in here.*

And then she heard Endora's mournful *meow* once again. The sound was coming from the bathroom.

She took a few more steps inside, puzzled over what the cat could possibly have gotten into.

She immediately discovered the reason for Endora's distress. She was in a molded-plastic cat carrier, which someone had placed in the bathtub.

Megan's stomach clenched at the sight of her locked up that way. But only a second or two passed before a feeling of horror came over her.

Who did this? she thought. Not the cleaning people. And if it was that guy Tom, why would he have put a cat in a bathtub?

The strangeness of what she had just found reminded her of her original mission: packing up her stuff, grabbing Endora, and getting out.

She leaned over the tub, planning to grab the cat carrier and run. But she stopped abruptly when she noticed a line of bottles and jars neatly lined up on the counter. Deodorant, makeup, body lotion . . . Each one brand new and unopened, some still in boxes or blister packs.

All of them the brands she used.

They were duplicates of the products she'd brought to the house. Even the shades were identical, she saw as she picked up a blister pack of L'Oreal blush labeled "Subtle Sable."

Understanding hit her like a bolt of lightning.

"Oh, my God!" she cried, her voice a hoarse whisper.

She dropped the package on the counter as if it was hot enough to sear her skin. Then noticed that among all the jars and bottles was an unopened tube of the special honeysuckle-scented shower gel, the one that was only available online.

And then one more item in the line-up caught her eye: a gold tube of lipstick.

She dashed out of the bathroom, feeling as if she was going to be sick. Her eyes darted around the bedroom, now seeing things differently.

Rushing over to the mini-fridge, she flung open the door. In it were several cartons of yogurt, milk, and eggs, all brands carried by Trader Joe's.

In the door was a bottle of Moet et Chandon.

As she slammed the refrigerator door, she glanced up and saw that lined up neatly on the shelf above was more food. A carton of butternut squash soup, a bottle of white wine, a bag of gingersnaps.

It was only then that she noticed the bouquet in the opposite corner, gracing a small table. A dozen yellow roses.

"Oh, my God!" she exclaimed.

She turned toward the door, then froze.

John was standing in the doorway.

"I've been waiting for you, Megan," he said calmly. "Welcome home."

She watched in horror as the door swung shut. Then let out a cry of utter despair as she heard the click of the lock.

CHAPTER 30

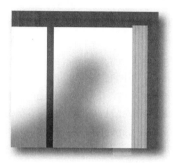

Megan rushed across the room and grasped the doorknob. Desperately she tried to turn it, pulling with every bit of strength she possessed. It didn't budge.

Oh, my God! she thought, her head buzzing as she tried to comprehend the fact that John had locked her in.

She told herself to calm down, that the worst thing she could do was panic.

Forcing herself to take deep breaths, she searched for her pocketbook, where her cell phone was. Then remembered that she'd left it in the bedroom.

She surveyed the room again. Only this time, she was looking for another way out.

She dashed over to the window and pulled up the blinds. Then let out a cry when she saw that this was no ordinary window. Not only was the glass reinforced by wire mesh; there was a steel band all around it, making it clear it wasn't meant to be opened.

Even so, she couldn't resist banging on the glass, then trying with all her strength to push it open. She gave up after only a few seconds, her mind flitting to another possibility.

The bathroom. Maybe there was a window in there.

As she rushed inside, she saw the cat carrier in the bathtub. But she didn't bother with Endora, despite the cat's pleading meows. Instead, she studied the walls.

It only took a second or two to see there was no window in here. Only a small vent that was built into the ceiling.

Of course there's no window, she thought woefully, shuffling back into the bedroom. She sank onto the bed, overwhelmed with despair. Letting the tears that had been welling up in her eyes stream down her cheeks.

Think, she commanded herself. Sooner or later, he'll be back. And whenever that happens, you have to be ready.

Once again her eyes darted around the room. Only this time she was looking for a weapon. Not the usual type, but some ordinary object that if used the right way would enable her overpower him, or at least get past him.

A lamp? A dinner plate? The bottle of champagne?

She even considered the microwave, but saw that it was bolted in place.

She wondered if there was a knife or a pair of scissors lying in a drawer. But she didn't bother to get up and look.

It was clear that he'd thought of everything. A jailer didn't leave scissors and knives in his prisoner's cell. And that was exactly what she was. A prisoner.

John had set a trap for her and she walked right into it.

He'd obviously put tremendous effort into planning it, too, ever since she moved in. Observing her. Learning about her. Finding out what foods she liked, her favorite type of champagne, the brands and even the exact shades of cosmetics she used.

The coziness of the room only added to the bizarreness of the situation. Bright yellow walls, the pretty bedspread, the bouquet of what used to be her favorite flower.

But there was no doubt that it was a jail cell. A room that was no more comfortable, no more appealing, than it would have been if it were made of concrete and cinderblocks.

Megan wrapped her arms around her waist protectively, trying to keep herself from panicking by constructing rationalizations.

He can't keep you here for long, she told herself. The idea of John holding someone captive here in his house is just too crazy. We're right outside one of the largest cities in the world, for heaven's sake, not some remote village or a farmhouse stuck out in the middle of nowhere.

Besides, someone is bound to come looking for me. Brenda or Elissa or Chloe . . .

She swiped at her eyes, which burned from the salt of her tears. She knew it would be days, even weeks, before her friends noticed her silence. And when they did, it was very possible they'd assume she was simply wrapped up in her writing and her luxurious house with a pool . . . or that she and Greg had reunited and were too enthralled with each other to bother with anyone else.

What about Greg? she thought, her despair temporarily lifting.

But it descended again as her parting words echoed in her head. "Don't call me again," she'd told him. *"Ever!"*

Russell? The flicker of hope that came from remembering her annoying neighbor was snuffed out fast. Only the day before she'd told him that if he set foot anywhere near John's house, she'd call the police.

Megan struggled to come up with other people who might come looking for her. She even considered the clerk at Speedy's. But while he was aware that she was housesitting—knew all about the ad on the bulletin board, in fact—he had never known John's address. Not even his last name. The clerk didn't have access to his phone number, either. Not since John went into the store and took down the ad.

The cleaning service? she thought, experiencing a momentary flash of hopefulness. Then realized they had never even existed. The same went for his friend Tom.

None of it had been real.

Eventually, someone will put two and two together, she told herself. My girlfriends or Greg . . . and when they do, they'll go to the police. They all know where I've been staying. All of them can give the cops this address.

Surely someone will come looking for me then.

Yet even that scenario wasn't very encouraging. She could picture John standing in the doorway, perfectly at ease as he chatted with a couple of cops who were about as interested as Officer Garcia was. She imagined John doing a completely convincing job of acting concerned but surprised. Insisting that Megan Quinn left his house ages ago, without leaving a forwarding address. Maybe even claiming she'd said something about going back home to Pennsylvania . . .

Besides, she thought morosely, who knows what will have happened by the time the police come looking for me?

Megan didn't know how much time passed before she jumped at the sound of metal scraping against metal. A key inserted into the lock, the tumblers turning . . . Instinctively she leaped to her feet.

Ready to fight.

"Knock, knock," John said pleasantly, opening the door a few inches and peering inside. "Mind if I come in?"

The banality of his question reinforced the feeling that she was in the middle of a nightmare. Desperately wishing she could wake up. She didn't answer. Instead, as he came into the room, she stood at attention, her hands clenched into fists.

Thinking, Maybe he's come back to let me out of here. To tell me all this is just his idea of a joke. The fact that he was carrying her suitcase added to her hopefulness.

But that feeling vanished as soon as he said, "I brought your things. They certainly won't do you any good out there!"

With the same cheerfulness, he added, "And you don't have to worry about your personal items, since I've stocked your bathroom with duplicates. I wanted to make sure you felt right at home. After all, you live here now."

He took a step toward her, and she recoiled.

Trying not to whimper, she begged, "Please don't hurt me."

"Hurt you?" John looked shocked. Putting down her suitcase, he said, "Why would I hurt you? That's the last thing I'd ever do!"

It was only then that she realized he was something worse than malevolent. He was completely insane. She could see it now, in his eyes. A distinctive look she couldn't quite find the right word for. Distracted? Disconnected?

Crazed?

She wondered if it had been there all along, and she'd simply never noticed.

He hovered a few feet away from her, his stance awkward and his hands fidgeting. She was relieved that he didn't come any closer.

"You never left, did you?" she said, her voice a hoarse whisper.

"Of course not," he replied, sounding matter-of-fact. "I'd never go far away from you, Megan. I couldn't bear that."

Her blood ran cold. A hundred questions, accusations, and demands roared in her head. But she remained silent, afraid of saying the wrong thing.

Afraid of making a horrendous, nearly-incomprehensible situation even worse.

"I figure you'll need some time to get settled," John went on, still just as upbeat. "But I thought we'd do something special for dinner tonight."

"Dinner?" she repeated, not able to believe he was talking about something so mundane.

"There's plenty of stuff in the refrigerator for your lunch," he said, gesturing toward the makeshift kitchen, "but we want our first dinner together to be memorable."

He frowned. "I've actually been a bit concerned about the way you've been eating. Really, Megan, soup and yogurt for dinner? I thought you said something about starting to cook yourself real meals."

"How do you know what I've been eating for dinner?" she demanded.

A look of surprise crossed his face, as if he could hardly believe she was asking such a silly question. "By going through your trash, of course. It's amazing what you can learn about a person's habits that way."

She stopped herself from crying out. Careful not to react, at least until she could figure out what was going on in his head and decide the best way to conduct herself.

"But all that will be different now," he continued. "Believe it or not, I'm actually a pretty good cook. I got tired of eating fast food and take-out a while ago, so I went out and bought myself some cookbooks. I'm not exactly a gourmet chef, but I can promise you three square meals a day."

His prattle about their life together, especially his apparent assumption that it would continue indefinitely, crushed her last lingering hopes that there was an easy way out of this. She was beginning to understand that logic didn't stand a chance.

From the bathroom came the sound of Endora's mewing, a desperate plea for help. The poor cat had undoubtedly heard John's voice and was appealing to someone she saw as another possible savior.

"I should get that animal out of here," John muttered, sounding as if he was talking to himself. "I don't know much about cats, but they strike me as creatures that don't like to be locked up."

Megan's head spun as she tried to come up with right comment, formulate the exact phrase that would make him see the lunacy of what he was doing and set her free, as well. But she was afraid of furthering his resolve. Or making him angry.

His insistence that the last thing he wanted to do is hurt her alarmed her, rather than comforting her.

He can't comprehend that he's hurting me simply by keeping me locked up.

She kept her eyes on him as he went into the bathroom. He had his back to her, making this a good time to attack him.

But she wasn't prepared. There was nothing in the room that could serve as a weapon. Nothing to stab him with, strangle him with, even hit him over the head with.

And while her daily swimming had strengthened all her muscles, she didn't know the first thing about fighting. Besides, he was so much bigger than she was. Six feet tall, at least, and in reasonably good shape.

Not exactly someone she could take on one-to-one and expect to debilitate.

John came out of the bathroom a few seconds later with the cat carrier. Endora was still voicing her displeasure over being his captive.

"I'll take her into the kitchen and give her some water," he said. "She must be pretty thirsty by now. And then I'll leave you alone for a while. Give you some time to get used to the place."

Beaming, he added, "And to start thinking about this as *our* house."

CHAPTER 31

He can't remember having ever been so happy before in his entire life. *I finally have the one thing I've always wanted,* John thinks, standing by the swimming pool and gazing at the calming blue water. *Someone whose entire focus is me.*

Who sees only me, thinks only of me, lives only for me.

Someone I can have all to myself.

He's waited so long for this. The chance to do it right. After what happened last time, he knew he'd need exactly the right circumstances.

Like owning a house.

His very own place, in a quiet neighborhood where no one knew him. In a city where no one paid much attention to anyone else.

The moment he learned that his grandmother had left him her house, he knew he finally had the setting he needed.

As for advertising for a housesitter, that was a brainstorm that had struck him soon after he'd moved in. He'd had the idea when he was driving around town and happened to pass the Pasadena Animal Shelter.

He'd met so many women and they were all so wrong. And then Megan had come along. He'd known from the start that she was perfect.

Pretty and smart and completely without pretense.

But she was also trusting. Sweet. Eager to please.

Perhaps even more importantly, she had few connections. Hardly anyone in her life who would notice right away that she was gone.

The right person.

And unlike with Caroline, John had given Megan more time. Time to get used to living in the house, time to feel at home. Time to think of his house as *her* house.

He's done everything possible to make her comfortable. Given her everything she needs to make her feel at home. Her favorite foods, the shampoo and the make-up she likes, the yellow roses she adores. Books and chocolates and other little surprises, hidden away in places where she's likely to stumble across them.

He knows it's only a question of time before she accepts her new living arrangements.

I chose well, he tells himself, experiencing a surge of satisfaction.

We really will live happily ever after.

CHAPTER 32

Time had come to a standstill. That was how Megan felt as she sat on the edge of the bed, trying not to panic. No clock in the room. No wristwatch. No cell phone, no computer, no television, no radio, no contact with the outside world. She had no way of knowing if minutes or hours passed. It felt like hours. But the sun remained in the sky, not budging.

She was doing absolutely nothing, yet could feel the energy draining out of her.

Reluctantly she lay down, pulling the bedspread over her and curling up in a ball. Afraid to stop standing guard, but desperately wanting to shut out what was happening.

She finally let herself cry.

Sobs wracked her body. Her shoulders shook, rasping, choking sounds bruised her throat. She stuffed the bedspread in her mouth, trying to muffle the noise.

How could I have been so blind? Why didn't I figure out what was going on?

And then: *Who would ever guess something like this could happen?*

A total stranger. Someone she'd only met twice.

Even then their interactions had been matter-of-fact. Looking each other over, exchanging basic information. A test for suitability, like a job interview.

At least, that was what she'd thought.

She agonized over her stupidity, her childlike willingness to trust. Yet as hard as she tried to blame herself, she couldn't identify a particular point at which she could have, *should* have, put all the pieces together.

Somehow she managed to drift off to sleep. At least that was what she realized when some time later she felt herself jerk awake.

Megan's eyes flew open. Her heart pounding, her senses on alert.

The room was dark, the only illumination the last lingering light of day that trickled through the window. Instantly she remembered everything. And dreaded confronting whatever awakened her.

Her worst fears were realized when she heard a key being inserted in the lock, followed by the sound of tumblers turning.

She bolted upright and clutched the blanket tightly against her as if it had the power to shield her. She fought the urge to whimper when a sliver of light exploded through the darkness. She shut her eyes. When she cautiously reopened them, she saw John's silhouette in the doorway.

"Hey, sleepyhead," he said, his voice soft and soothing. "I'm glad you got some rest, but it's time to get up."

He snapped on the overhead light. As her eyes adjusted, she saw that he was carrying a tray piled high with food, plates, even a yellow rose in a vase. Carefully folded fabric that looked like a tablecloth was draped over one arm. He walked toward her, and instinctively she shrank against the pillows.

He sat down on the edge of the bed.

"I told you we'd do something special for dinner," he said, his voice once again alarmingly cheerful. "But instead of cooking, I went to Bristol Farms and got take-out. I bought a bunch of different things, since it's going to take me a while to learn all your likes and dislikes. I got chicken salad, tequila shrimp, some amazing blue cheese and walnut crostini."

The matter-of-fact way in which he conveyed this information horrified her.

He really is acting as if this is a perfectly ordinary situation, she thought. As if we're friends or roommates . . .

Or lovers.

"It sounds wonderful," she said, doing her best to sound sincere. "But wouldn't it be more fun if we ate in the dining room? Or by the pool?"

His expression hardened. "I don't think you're ready for that."

"Okay," she said quickly. "Whatever you want."

She turned her eyes to the food, not wanting to look at him—or to let him see her disappointment.

"That looks amazing," she told him. "I'm starving."

"I'm so glad I picked things you like!" he said. She could practically feel how relieved he was.

He wants me to like him, she thought. Wondering if she could use his eagerness to please to her advantage.

"I thought we'd eat right here on the bed," he told her. "We can pretend we're having a picnic."

She was tempted to point out they could have had a *real* picnic by eating outside.

John spread the tablecloth out on the bed, then arranged the food on it. Megan was dismayed to see that he'd thought of everything—napkins, salt and pepper, serving spoons—eliminating the need for him to run out to get some forgotten item and possibly leaving the door ajar.

As she lifted a forkful of food to her mouth, she was surprised to discover how hungry she was.

"This is really good," she said sincerely.

"Bristol Farms is great," he replied. "Not cheap, but worth the splurge. Especially for a big occasion like this. Have you ever shopped there?" His tone was conversational, as if a captor and his captive dining on shrimp and chicken salad in a locked bedroom was the most ordinary situation in the world.

"No," she said. Then: "But I'd love to see it. Maybe we can go there together sometime."

He stiffened. "You can tell me what you're in the mood for and I can pick it up for you. I'll get their take-out menu the next time I'm there."

"They probably have a website, too," Megan ventured, aware that she was testing his limits.

When he didn't respond, didn't even look at her, she understood that she'd just overstepped them.

"I'm glad we're finally getting a chance to talk," she said quickly, desperate to gain his favor again. "Now that I've had a chance to live here in your beautiful house."

"Our house," he corrected her with a gentle smile.

Even though her throat had thickened, she forced herself to swallow another bite of food.

"How long have you lived here?" she asked.

"Since June."

She nearly choked. "So you just bought this place a few months ago?"

"Not exactly," John replied. "I inherited it. It was my grandmother's. She left it to me. And if the house itself wasn't enough of a windfall, she was in the process of renovating it when she died last spring. It was almost done, too, aside from a few finishing touches."

John's grandmother. Images from the first few days she'd spent in the house flashed into Megan's mind, discoveries that at the time didn't seem to form a pattern but now made perfect sense. The vintage clock next to the bed. The hot-water bottle. The ancient copper teakettle stashed away in a kitchen cabinet.

"In fact," John continued," my grandmother left me everything she had. That means we don't have to worry about money, Megan. Not ever."

Finding out that her captor was financially independent made Megan feel as if she'd just been punched in the stomach. That meant John had no need for a job. There was nothing that would force him to leave the house, to regularly interact with people who might pick up on his strange behavior or an accidental reference to the woman in his house.

She nodded dumbly, so stunned that she needed a few moments to recover.

"Where did you live before?" she finally asked.

"You're asking an awful lot of questions," he said, sounding irritated.

"I'm sorry. It's just that there are so many things I want to know." Nearly choking on her words, she added, "About you."

His expression was wary as he said, "We have plenty of time to get to know each other, Megan. All the time in the world."

When they finished eating, he gathered up the plates and the remaining food and piled everything back onto the tray.

"Please let me help," she offered.

"Not tonight," he said. "Tonight is too special."

Her stomach wrenched as she wondered what else he had planned for the evening.

But she was more concerned about the fact that she was starting to feel strange. Drowsy. Oddly disconnected. At first, she assumed she'd simply eaten too much. But this feeling of fatigue wasn't like anything she was used to. Her thoughts became clouded and her limbs were starting to feel as if they were no longer attached.

Her voice sounded far away as she said, "I think I have to lie down."

"Whatever you want, Megan," John said. "Whatever you need to be happy."

She opened her mouth to reply, but speaking was too difficult. As she felt herself being sucked into a thick sleep, she was only vaguely aware of the already-familiar sound of tumblers locking into place.

She was shocked that when she opened her eyes, sunlight was streaming into the room.

It's morning, she realized. Which means I slept through the entire night.

As she struggled to emerge from her groggy state, she concluded that she had probably been drugged.

A feeling of panic shot through her.

"Oh, no!" She whispered the words, afraid he'd hear her. Anxiously she slid her hands along her body. Taking inventory. Her clothes seemed intact, exactly as they were the night before. No buttons undone, her shirt still mostly tucked into her waistband. Her jeans zipped all the way up.

She exhaled, overcome with relief. But that relief was short-lived.

So nothing had happened—yet. But the bottom line was that she was still locked up in a crazy man's house, more puzzled than ever about what he wanted from her.

She turned to face the window, anxious to feel the warmth of the sunlight on her face. And immediately inhaled sharply.

The sheets on the other side of the bed were rumpled, just a little, as if someone had attempted to smooth them. And the pillow next to hers curved with a barely-perceptible indentation.

She was trying to convince herself that she was simply imagining things when on the crisp yellow pillowcase she spotted a single dark blond hair, the same shade as John's.

CHAPTER 33

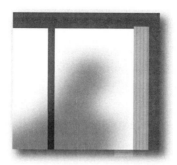

Two days passed, then three. Megan kept count, measuring the passage of time by the steady arrival of breakfast, lunch and dinner. The food always nicely arranged on a tray, accompanied by a yellow rose in a vase.

Food that she knew would be treacherous to eat.

She had to stay alert, couldn't allow herself to be drugged.

She had discovered with great relief that the jars and boxes on the shelf and in the refrigerator were still sealed, a sign they hadn't been tampered with. She filled up on yogurt and cookies and cheese when she was alone. Picked at her plate when John was in the room, nibbling the fruit and bread and other foods she thought were probably safe.

Making excuses for her selectivity: she had a stomachache, she didn't like mayonnaise, she was allergic to tomatoes.

John's eagerness to please continued to be an asset. He seemed surprised by her eating habits, then resigned. But every once in a while, she saw a suspicious look flicker across his face.

Every night, before going to sleep, Megan strewed the clothes she'd worn that day on the floor. Haphazardly, as if she'd simply tossed them there. She left her shoes in the middle of the room, where he was likely to trip over them in the dark. Then she piled the throw pillows in front of the door, carefully placing a ceramic mug and a drinking glass on top, an inch apart from each other. Figuring that if he came into the room, they would knock against each other as they fell, waking her before he reached the bed.

She kept one of her high-heeled shoes under the pillow.

But John didn't make any more nighttime visits. While Megan was relieved, she was also aware that it was most likely because he knew she wasn't ingesting the drugs.

He didn't seem to have thought up another way of keeping her compliant. At least, not yet.

Megan was determined not to become compliant again. She told herself over and over again that she could outsmart him. That she could escape.

That she *would* escape.

She remained in a heightened state, fueled by the adrenaline incessantly surging through her body. Constantly agonizing over how to get out.

When she was alone, she prowled around the room like a caged animal. Still looking for a way out. Ruminating about ways of tricking him or changing his mind or even incapacitating him, whatever it took to escape from this house that had become her prison.

In the meantime, she struggled to hold onto her sanity by clinging to little things that gave her some small measure of comfort. She took three or four showers a day. With so few ways of experiencing pleasure, she'd come to crave the feeling of steaming hot water pounding against her skin, the familiar smell of the honeysuckle shower gel. Sometimes, for a fleeting moment, she was able to forget.

She also worked at focusing on whatever shreds of normalcy she could find. Relishing the sweetness of a spoonful of yogurt, concentrating on the softness of the pillow beneath her head, losing herself in a fictional character's dilemma as she read one of the novels he'd brought her.

She constantly discovered small surprises he'd left for her. A stack of novels under the bathroom sink. Belgian chocolates in back of the refrigerator. Under the bed, a one thousand piece jigsaw puzzle, the picture on the box a harbor crowded with yachts that were ready to carry their lucky owners off to sea. She wondered if he was aware of the irony of contrasting the boaters' freedom with her total lack of it.

Whenever John was around, she acted as if she'd accepted the situation. She knew he was paying close attention to every word she uttered, monitoring her every move.

She was convinced that her best chance for getting out was making him believe she was happy. That sooner or later, he'd let down his guard enough for her to make her move. Or that she'd think of a way to make that happen.

On the third day, the idea struck her.

She was sitting on the floor, idly fingering the puzzle pieces she'd scattered over the carpet. Lost in thought, trying to anticipate how else John might try to sedate her.

It was at that moment that the thought popped into her head. Something so obvious she couldn't believe she hadn't thought of it before.

While John was watching *me*, she realized, I was watching *him*. Learning things about him, things most people wouldn't know, simply by living in the same space he lives in.

A plan quickly began to take form.

And for the first time since she'd become John's prisoner, Megan felt something that resembled hope.

CHAPTER 34

A s soon as John walked into the bedroom late in the afternoon of the fourth day, Megan sensed that something was different. He seemed calmer than usual. More relaxed. She wondered if it was simply that he'd become comfortable with their routine, that he believed she'd accepted the fact that from now on, this was how the two of them would live.

She was certain that was the case when he said, "You know, Megan, I feel really good about all this."

Measuring her words carefully, she replied, "Things seem to be going well, don't they?"

He looked pleased. Even smiled.

"My thoughts exactly," he said. "In fact, I've decided to let you out."

Out. Simply hearing the word sent adrenaline flooding through her veins.

And then she had an idea.

"Can I go swimming?" she asked, unable to hide her eagerness.

The idea of being outside was suddenly irresistible. To feel the sun on her skin, to breathe in fresh air . . .

And to have a chance to escape. Scramble over the fence, storm the gate, make a run for it no matter what the risks.

His expression hardened. "No," he said simply. "Not yet."

All hope drained out of her. But she'd become a master of hiding her true feelings.

"I'm sure whatever you've got planned will be great," she told him.

She was astonished by how excited she was over simply walking through the bedroom door.

Freedom, she thought giddily.

Her euphoria deflated as soon as he grabbed her arm. Holding onto her. *Tightly.*

Even inside the house, he wouldn't let her move around without him being in control. She shuffled down the hall alongside him, disappointed when he stopped in front of the master bedroom.

He let go of her arm and motioned for her to go inside.

As soon as she stepped into the bedroom, a wave of dizziness came over her.

Yellow roses were everywhere. Four or five bouquets, their scent overpowering.

But what horrified her even more were the rose petals. Dozens of them, strewn across the bed.

Which had been carefully turned down, the flowered sheets forming a perfect rectangle against the bedspread.

Her eyes darted around the room. Lighting on the bottle of Moet and the two champagne glasses on the night table. The lit candles lined up on the dresser, clustered together next to the bed.

Frantically she checked the French doors. Then couldn't help gasping when she saw the hefty chain woven through the handles, the ends clamped together with a padlock.

She turned and saw him watching her expectantly.

She forced herself to smile. "Wow. Everything looks so—"

"Romantic?" he asked, studying her face.

"Yes, romantic." Her mouth was so dry she could barely get the words out.

I have to get out of here, she thought for the thousandth time. But this time, with a sense of urgency she'd never felt before.

The fact that she was here in this room also brought her hope. The feeling was rooted in the idea that had been simmering at the back of her mind. The possibility, however small, that something she discovered about John while living in his house could help her gain the upper hand—at least long enough to get away.

It was time to find out.

"Do you know what I'd really like?" she asked, lowering her voice in an attempt at sounding seductive.

John's face lit up. "Anything," he said. "Whatever you want."

She gestured toward the bathroom off the master bedroom. "I'd adore a hot bath. The Jacuzzi is so amazing. You wouldn't mind, would you?"

When he didn't respond, she added, "It'll help me relax."

He thought for a second or two, then finally said, "Okay. I guess that wouldn't hurt."

She flashed him another smile then slipped into the bathroom. She shut the door, wondering if she dared lock it. Then quickly realized that John probably had a key.

Besides, the last thing she wanted was to make him suspicious.

She turned on both bathtub faucets, full force, wanting to make sure they made as much noise as possible. Then pulled off her shirt and pants. If he unexpectedly flung open the door, she wanted to make sure she looked as if she was in the middle of getting undressed.

Despite the backdrop of the rushing water, she was careful to be as quiet as possible as she opened the top drawer of the vanity. She kept checking the door, terrified it would open.

Even though the door remained closed, her breaths were fast and shallow. Her heart thumped loudly in her chest as she sorted through the plastic prescription bottles. When she located the one that contained the prednisone, she tucked it away beneath a washcloth left lying on the counter. Then she silently slid open the medicine cabinet, took out one of her bottles of pills, and screwed off the lid.

If he comes in, she thought, I'll tell him I forgot to take my vitamins today.

Quickly she opened the prescription bottle. She remembered that only a few days ago, it had been practically filled with the round white pills. Now, it was a little over half full, a sign that he'd been taking them regularly.

She poured the prednisone into her hand and counted the tablets. Then she counted out the same number of vitamin C tablets, which were nearly identical, round and white and approximately the same size. She switched the pills, filling the small plastic bottle with the vitamins and dumping the prednisone tablets into the vitamin bottle. When she was done, she put both bottles back where they were before.

Quickly she wriggled out of her bra and underpants, tested the water in the tub with her foot, and climbed into it. As she lowered herself into the steaming water, she let out her breath with the same force as the water gushing from the faucet.

She lay completely still, expecting to feel better over having taken action— any action. Instead, whatever optimism she'd dared to feel up to this point, whatever fantasies she'd entertained about being able to affect John's behavior, had faded.

It won't work, a voice inside her head taunted. Switching the pills isn't going to make a bit of difference.

Megan was even more tense than before when she came back into the bedroom, her skin still damp beneath her clothes. Not just because of what she'd done but because she now had to deal with what John had planned.

He was standing in the doorway, a formidable obstacle between the bedroom and the rest of the world.

"Did you enjoy your bath?" he asked.

"It was great," she told him, knowing that was the right answer. "Exactly what I needed."

He gave a satisfied nod. "Good."

Standing awkwardly before him, she glanced around the room.

"You really thought of everything," she said, stalling.

He smiled. "I did, didn't I."

And then: "Why don't you get comfortable?"

Panic rose up inside her. She fought the feeling, knowing that giving in to it would only make her even more vulnerable.

You just have to get through this, she told herself. Pretend you're not even here. Focus on something else, make yourself believe you're far, far away . . .

Gingerly she perched on the edge of the bed. And then she spotted it.

Her laptop, sitting on the dresser.

Immediately her heartbeat sped up. It was so fast and so loud she was afraid he could hear it pounding in her chest. She wondered if he read her ramblings, her thoughts about Greg and her life . . .

And him.

None of that mattered now. Instead, she saw her computer as the chance she'd been waiting for. Hoping for.

Desperately.

"You know," she said casually, "I'd really love something to drink. That hot bath made me thirsty."

"There's champagne," he said with pride. "I got your favorite kind."

"That's for later," she said. "Right now, my throat is so dry. Anything cold would be great."

He thought for a moment. "I have ginger ale."

"Perfect. With ice, please. Lots of ice."

She wished she could have come up with a more elaborate recipe. One that would take even longer to prepare. But she'd have to work with what she had. Which meant moving fast.

"Ginger ale it is," John said. He trotted off to the kitchen, but not before closing the bedroom door and locking it with a loud *snap*.

Megan was ready. As soon as he was gone, she dashed over to the laptop and opened it. The screen was dark. She pressed the power button and waited.

I'll email Brenda, she thought. Chloe or Elissa might simply freak out. They might not know what to do—or even whether or not to believe me.

But Brenda was bound to be good in a crisis. She worked with pregnant women, for heaven's sake.

Her laptop seemed to be taking forever to boot up.

"Come on, come on . . ."

She mouthed the words without actually saying anything, afraid he'd hear her. Her eyes darted back and forth between the screen and the doorway. Through the closed door she could hear the sounds of the refrigerator closing, of ice tumbling into a glass.

And then the familiar wallpaper appeared on the laptop screen, the blue sky with puffy clouds that signified the perfect day. She clicked the Internet icon, and a few seconds later Google popped up. Commanding her hand to remain steady, she clicked on Gmail.

The sight of all the emails people had sent her over the past few days almost made her cry out with relief. She hadn't been forgotten. There were people out there who were trying to communicate with her. But she didn't have time to see who they were, what they were saying. She clicked Compose Mail.

The New Message screen came up.

Steady. You can do this.

She willed her shaking hands to type: B—R—E—N—D—A—2—2—2 @ . . .

The sound of the bedroom door opening had barely registered before she heard, "What do you think you're doing?"

His voice cut through her like fingernails on a chalkboard.

She glanced up and saw him standing in the doorway, a glass in one hand.

His face stricken.

"I just wanted to—"

"Give me that!" He rushed toward her, spilling the ginger ale. He set the glass down on the dresser, then lunged for the laptop.

"No!" she cried. "It's mine!"

She was closer so she got to it first. In one fluid gesture, she grabbed it with both hands, shut the lid, and swung it through the air. Aiming for his head, feeling her own power as adrenaline surged through her, giving her superhuman strength. But before she could make contact, she felt his hands clamp around her wrists, freezing her arms in mid-air.

She cried out, shocked by how quickly he'd moved, how easily he'd stopped her. Still trying to understand what was happening when he let go of her and snatched away the computer. Everything else blocked out by incomprehensible pain as hard molded plastic struck her skull.

Flashing lights. A loud buzzing. The frightening jolt inside her head, as if her brain had become dislodged.

She crumpled to the floor, only vaguely aware that the animal-like moan that sounded so far away was actually coming from her.

Wanting only to retreat, to curl up on the carpet, to find a way to stop the explosion inside her head. Her muscles limp, unable to resist being roughly yanked to her feet. As he dragged her away—out of the room, back to her prison—she broke into sobs, the last of her energy seeping away.

With it, every last bit of hope.

It's just like last time, he tells himself, fury rising up inside him.

Megan is screaming so loudly that John has to clamp one hand over her mouth as he hauls her back to her room. His other arm is wrapped around her waist and arms, half-carrying her as she drags her feet on the carpet.

Refusing to cooperate.

Hitting him with the realization that she'll never cooperate.

He's nearly overwhelmed with disappointment.

I thought I could trust her, he thinks, trying to block out the sound of her screams so he can think. That I could make her care about me.

That this time I'd get it right, that it would work out the way I wanted.

But no. The entire scenario is playing out the same way it did with Caroline.

Once he's pushed her into the bedroom, he slams the door and turns the lock, testing it to make sure it's secure. Then he goes back to the master bedroom, where he blows out the candles.

Extinguishing the flames seems to extinguish any last lingering traces of hope.

John pulls a key out of its hiding place, unlocks the French doors, and goes outside, into the backyard. He can still hear her pounding on the door, screaming so loudly that her voice is becoming raw.

He closes the French doors, worried that her voice will carry, glad no neighbors are nearby. Feeling overwhelmed, he sinks into a chair next to the pool and stares at the calm blue water.

I love her, he thinks, his mind reeling. I've done everything for Megan. But she still refuses to do the only thing I've ever wanted of her: to love me back.

As difficult as it is to accept, he knows his expectations have to change. That he has to get used to the fact that he's not going to get his happily ever after ending.

But then there's the problem of what to do about Megan. He knows that if he sets her free, she'll tell.

Just like Caroline.

Only this time, he can't let it end the same way. The idea of being sent somewhere like The Lost Place is unbearable.

Which means one thing: he can never let Megan leave.

Chapter 35

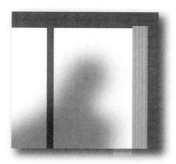

Another day passed. But it wasn't the delivery of meals that told Megan how much time had gone by. There had been no meals. No dinner the night before, after John had dragged her back to her room and locked her in again. No breakfast that morning. No lunch, either. There had been no sign of John at all, in fact.

She began to wonder if he'd simply left her here. Forgotten about her.

Or maybe he was punishing her.

She was even more on edge than usual as she paced around the room. Waiting, simply waiting, even though she had no idea what she was waiting for. She kept her strength up by doing what she'd been doing almost since the beginning: snacking on the food in the room.

When the sunlight appeared to be waning, some time late in the afternoon, she heard the familiar scraping of metal against metal.

A key in the lock.

Instinctively she leaped to her feet. For a fleeting moment, almost allowing herself to believe that someone had come to save her. Instead, the door opened and John came into the room.

Her heart sank.

"Hello, Megan," he said, his voice flat.

Almost immediately she noticed that he seemed different. Distracted. Disoriented, even. His eyes dull, his skin pale, his shoulders stooped.

Megan experienced a flutter of hope, her heartbeat quickening as she ran through the list she remembered from the website.

Weakness, extreme fatigue, nausea, vomiting, diarrhea. Dizziness, fainting, slowed movements. Drop in blood sugar, drop in blood pressure. Joint pain, stomach pain, muscle aches, fever, weight loss.

Occasionally, changes in mental state.

The symptoms of prednisone withdrawal.

She opened her mouth, prepared to play her usual role. Sweet. Pliant. Caring.

To ask how he was feeling, perhaps to remark that he didn't look well. But before she had a chance to speak, John brought around the arm he'd been holding behind his back.

She stifled a cry, expecting something frightening. A gun, a knife, a rope, or a hundred other horrifying possibilities.

Then gasped in surprise when she saw what he'd brought her.

Her bathing suit.

She realized that she hadn't had time to pack any of her suits. Had forgotten about them, in fact, since they were all damp and hung over the shower to dry.

This one was the most modest suit she owned, the navy blue tank suit.

"I've got good news for you, Megan," John told her, his voice strangely far-away. "You're finally getting what you wanted. You're going for a swim."

As Megan moved along the hallway, her movements were wooden, her breaths short and shallow. She was terrified by not knowing what John had planned for her.

She kept thinking about the movie Greg had mentioned, the one about zombies. *Night of the Living Dead.* Just thinking about the title made her shudder.

Yet something gave her encouragement.

Beside her, John was also walking slowly. Instead of his usual pace—what you'd expect of a tall, fit, 40-year-old man—he barely lifted his feet. While he clutched her arm with one hand, he ran the other along the wall, keeping his arm low so she wouldn't notice. As if he needed support. Or balance.

And then, suddenly, he slumped against the wall, hitting it with his shoulder. He let out a soft moan, rubbed his eyes with his free hand.

Megan's heartbeat quickened.

Dizziness, fainting, slowed movements. Drop in blood sugar, drop in blood pressure . . .

It's working, she thought triumphantly. He's going through drug withdrawal. I tricked him. Like he tricked me.

"Are you all right?" she asked, doing her best to sound concerned.

"I'm fine," he insisted. His voice vague and far away.

She warned herself to keep her giddiness in check. While switching his pills from prednisone to vitamins had clearly put a dent in the physical advantage he had over her, she still had no way of knowing if his weakened state would be to her benefit.

Not when she had no idea what he had planned.

As she passed through the French doors and outside onto the patio, the sun's lingering warmth embraced her. She turned her face upward, wishing she could luxuriate in it. Instead, she wondered if this was the last time she would ever feel the sun on her skin.

She remembered all the other times she'd taken this same route. The bright mornings and the lazy afternoons when she'd headed out to the pool, anticipating the exhilarating experience ahead, feeling liberated by wearing nothing but a bathing suit.

Today, wearing a bathing suit made her feel even more vulnerable.

When they reached the pool, John finally let go of her arm.

"Go ahead," he told her. "Jump in."

His voice still softer than usual. More distant. As if he was having trouble focusing.

She felt another surge of optimism.

Megan could feel his eyes upon her as she stood at the edge of the pool, next to the diving board. She looked down, noticing how the clear turquoise ripples glistened in the sunlight.

As if the water was completely benign.

She dove in, surprised that this time felt like every other time. She started to swim, quickly hitting her stride. Falling into a comfortable rhythm, as usual taking pleasure in the strength of her muscles as she glided effortlessly through the water. When she reached the end, she turned to do another lap, wishing she could go on forever.

She tried to forget he was watching her.

Yet every time she raised her head to breathe, she saw the blurry image of John standing by the pool.

His hand was pressed against his forehead. At first she thought he was shielding his eyes from the sun, the better to follow her every movement. Then wondered if it was something more. Something that was related to his reduced functioning. *Weakness, extreme fatigue, dizziness* . . .

She swam a few more laps, noticing that she was starting to tire. She suspected the unnatural tension in her muscles had sapped some of their energy.

She stopped at the deep end, poking her head up above the surface, her arms and legs still moving as she treaded water.

"Keep going!" John yelled.

She understood then what he was doing. Trying to exhaust her. To weaken her.

To make it more difficult for her to put up a fight.

She kept swimming, but more slowly, exerting as little energy as possible. Her arms gliding gently through the water, her legs kicking listlessly, barely moving at all.

Back and forth, back and forth.

She surfaced again, anxious to see John's reaction. When she swiped the water out of her eyes, her stomach clenched.

He was no longer standing in the same spot. In his place was a pile of clothes.

She whirled around, confusion ratcheting up her fear.

And then she saw him: poised at the edge of the deep end, about to dive in. Wearing a bathing suit he must have had on under his pants.

A tremendous splash of water. He was in the pool with her.

He swam over, treading water once he was close. Then surprised her by saying, "This is fun, isn't it?"

"Yes," she agreed readily.

"That's what I wanted, Megan. For us to have fun together."

"We *do* have fun," she insisted.

"But I wanted more than that," he said, strangely calm. "I wanted you to care for me."

"I do care for you!" she cried.

"That's a lie!" His voice sharp now. "If you did, you wouldn't try to leave. You'd be happy staying here in the house with me."

"I *am* happy!"

He acted as if he hadn't heard her. "You'll never stop trying to get away from me. I know that now."

"Then let me go!" she begged. "Please, let me walk away. Right now. We can still be friends. I'll come see you whenever you want. And I won't tell anyone. I promise!"

"You know I can't let you leave, Megan," John said, his voice once again emotionless. "Not today. Not ever."

She was about to protest, to try to find words that could change his mind. But before she could speak, she felt his hands on her shoulders, pushing her downward.

Her instinct was to scream.

But all too quickly she was beneath the water's surface, her scream dissolving into nothing more than a gasp. She fought back, struggling to push him away.

She could tell he was much weaker than he'd been that day in the master bedroom, when she'd tried to hit him with her laptop. Then, he'd overpowered her easily. Now, however, she was almost an even match for him. Even so, he was able to hold her under, wrapping his arms around her tightly as if to crush her.

Megan fought the urge to panic, the feelings of terror that came from being submerged. There was no air to inhale, only the greedy water shoving its way into her nose and her mouth, determined to make it impossible for her to breathe. As she struggled, she could feel the muscles of her arms and legs growing weaker and weaker.

First and foremost was the urge to breathe, the horrifying nightmare experience of craving air when there was none.

She suddenly remembered that when you were drowning, your whole life was supposed to flash before your eyes. But one particular day was coming back to her, as real as if she was living through it all over again.

Late August, at the beach with her family. Ellie's family, too, her parents and her two brothers. Megan and Ellie were the youngest of the group, only two years apart, close enough in age that the grown-ups were always trying to pair them off.

"You two go play in the water," Megan's mother insisted distractedly, already absorbed in spreading out blankets and unpacking cold drinks.

Ellie brightened. "C'mon, Megan, let's race!"

Reluctantly, Megan followed her older cousin into the surf. Took a few seconds to get used to its coolness, then jumped in, relishing the sense of freedom she always got from being in the water.

She swam out to where the water was deep enough that she couldn't stand. Anxious to put some distance between herself and the rest of her family. Wanting to enjoy the water—alone.

But instead of Ellie ignoring her, as she'd hoped, she swam up beside her. Stopping a few feet away, treading water. Splashing water in Megan's face, laughing every time she dowsed her.

"Hey, let's play a game!" Ellie cried.

Her suggestion made Megan cringe. Ellie never paid any attention to her except when she was in the mood to torment her. Never when the grown-ups were around, of course. She always waited until the two of them were alone. Then she would jab her with her finger. Pull her hair. Pinch her until she screamed, then berate her for acting like a baby.

"C'mon, Megan!" Ellie whined, splashing more water in her face. "Play with me!"

"Leave me alone! I'd rather swim."

"Don't be such a baby!" The same accusation as always, hurled in the same jeering tone.

"Ellie, leave me alone!" Megan glanced toward the shoreline, hoping to see one of the adults wading in. But they were clustered together on the beach, most of them with their backs to the water.

"Hey, I have an idea!" Ellie exclaimed, swimming over to her. "Let's play shark!"

"I don't want to." Megan's voice feeble this time. Already knowing she didn't have much choice. Not when the two of them were alone out here. Out of earshot, away from the grown-ups' view.

"C'mon, you dork, shark is a great game," Ellie insisted. "It'll be fun!"

"How do you play?" Megan asked warily.

Already resigned to doing whatever her older cousin wanted, she hoped that going along would keep her from devising some new way of torturing her.

But her stomach was in knots. Ellie on land was bad enough. Ellie in the ocean was something else entirely. Megan was a pretty good swimmer, but the water out here was a few inches over her head.

Not deep. But deep enough.

"Okay, so here's how you play," Ellie said, clearly comfortable about taking charge. "You're the girl who's swimming and I'm the shark. You can't see me because I'm under the water."

"I don't think I—"

But Ellie had already dived under the surface. Megan could see her heading toward her, her arms and legs squiggly masses. Longingly she looked at the shoreline again. Not understanding this game, but sensing that it wasn't a *good* game.

Not if Ellie had invented it.

And then she felt Ellie grab her around her legs. Preventing her from kicking, from keeping herself afloat. Pulling her down, the older girl strong enough that forcing Megan under the water was easy.

"Ellie!" She tried to scream her name, but opening her mouth only forced salt water in as she plunged downward.

How long did Ellie hold her under? She didn't know how many seconds passed, only that it was much too long. Some primitive survival mechanism kicked in, causing her to thrash around desperately, struggling to wrest herself away from Ellie's grip.

When she was finally able to breathe again, it wasn't because she managed to break away but because her tormentor had finally decided to release her.

"You are such a baby!" Ellie shrieked, treading water once again, closer than before. "*Ba*-by! *Ba*-by!"

Her taunting voice, the glint in her eyes . . . Megan knew Ellie expected her to start crying. Or to swim away in defeat. Giving in, like always, allowing her cousin to do whatever she wanted.

This time, things were different. *She* felt different.

"My turn!" Megan cried. "Now *I'm* the shark!"

Perhaps it was because she had a confidence in the water she didn't have on land. Or maybe something in her had snapped. But she surprised herself by lunging toward Ellie, grasping her by the shoulders. Catching her off-guard, before her cousin had a chance to fight back. Before she could even take a deep breath.

Megan was surprised by how easily she went down. By how little strength it took to hold her below the water's surface.

She could feel Ellie fighting back, trying to get away. But instead of letting go, she climbed on top of her shoulders, straddling her neck. Using all her weight to hold her under the water.

It seemed as if Ellie struggled for a long time. Megan held on, determined not to let her cousin get the best of her, just this once. Then was surprised when Ellie stopped fighting. Stopped moving completely, in fact, her limp body finally slipping away from beneath her.

"Okay, you can come out now," Megan shouted, swimming away. "Game's over."

She continued treading water. Watching the spot where Ellie had been, waiting for her to surface. Triumphant, this time, giddy over having finally fought back.

Growing angry, at first, when Ellie didn't pop her head out. As if she was being stubborn, refusing to do what Megan wanted her to do.

"Ellie?" she called, her voice wavering. Knowing her cousin couldn't hear her, not with her head still under the water. "*Ellie?*"

Not angry anymore. But a sense of uneasiness had come over her.

Megan glanced at the beach, where the adults and the other cousins were now sprawled out on blankets. Ignoring the two girls in the water as they slathered lotion on each other's shoulders and passed around cans of soda. She scanned the group, wondering if somehow, magically, she'd spot Ellie among them.

When she didn't, she looked back at the spot where her cousin had been. And saw her floating, facedown, on the water's surface.

A wave of satisfaction rose up inside her as she thought, Now she won't bother me anymore. That feeling vanished when a second later she heard a scream.

"Ellie!"

Megan snapped her head sideways and saw that all the members of her family were suddenly on their feet, their eyes fixed on the water. Three of the adults, her father and Ellie's parents, were racing to the water, jumping in and swimming toward her.

She was struck by the fact that her uncle hadn't stopped to take off the goofy Hawaiian shirt he'd had on all morning. In fact, she decided she was going to make a joke about it, once he got close. But when the three grown-ups reached her, she could tell from his expression that he wasn't in a joking mood.

"Ellie!" her aunt shrieked. "My baby!"

"My God!" Her uncle grabbed his daughter's flaccid body and pressed his mouth against hers, making choking noises like sobs as he tried to breathe life back into her.

"Megan!" her father gasped, seizing her by the shoulders. "What the hell happened?"

"I don't know!" she wailed, now crying herself. More upset by her father's anger than by the sight of her lifeless cousin. "We were playing around, that's all! She wanted to prove she could stay under longer than me!"

Suddenly Megan clamped her mouth shut, realizing she had to be careful. That if she said the wrong thing, nothing would ever be the same.

That happened anyway.

"No one blames you, Megan," her parents said over and over again in the weeks that followed.

That was what the therapist kept saying, too. And everyone else who insisted they were trying to help. But the very fact that they *said* it—felt they *needed* to say it—told her that deep down they had their suspicions. That even though they didn't know what had happened that day, the fact that she hadn't saved Ellie, hadn't even screamed for help, meant that she had to bear at least some responsibility for what happened.

Her therapist told her repeatedly that her goal was to help her put the incident behind her. And Megan did, although she always suspected it was more because she hadn't really cared about what had happened to Ellie than because of any professional expertise.

But the one thing she never forgot, the part that stuck with her, was how good it had felt to finally get revenge. To turn the tables on her tormenter, to be the one who triumphed in the end.

That feeling suddenly came back to her, as real as it had been that day in August.

A jolt of electricity shot through her, recharging her muscles. Recharging her resolve. All I have to do, Megan thought, is pick the right moment. She ran over the details of that long ago day, viewing them differently. Objectively.

Remembering the way Ellie's body had gone limp.

Even though John was still pushing her under the water, she forced herself to stop resisting. Fought the instinctive urge to struggle against her attacker, instead relaxing every one of her muscles.

Only a few seconds passed before John's grip loosened.

She remained still. The water's movement telling her he was swimming away.

She waited only another second or two, then with a violent splash shot out of the water, her rage giving her the strength to catapult high into the air.

Letting out a savage yell, she clamped both her hands on his head, digging her fingers into his scalp. His weakened state, combined with the full force of her weight as she jumped him from above, enabled her to throw him off balance. To force him under the water's surface.

To hold him there, even as he struggled. Fighting her, but with much less force than before.

Her teeth clenched, a deep, guttural sound like a growl emerging from her throat, Megan held her ground. She was hyper-aware of the fury surging through her, the adrenaline that fueled her with almost super-human strength.

And then his body slackened. She still held on to him, waiting. Wanting to be sure.

Finally letting go.

She stared at his motionless body, drifting through the water right in front of her, his arms and legs awkwardly awry.

Watching, just watching.

All sense of time had vanished. Perhaps seconds passed, perhaps minutes. The rest of the world reduced to the sound of her own breathing, now low and even.

She was completely numb, as if all her emotions had shut down.

Until relief flowed through her like a calming drug, along with the understanding that she was free.

Epilogue

Six Weeks Later

Megan stepped into the elevator, checking her watch to make sure she wasn't late. Two minutes to ten. As usual, she was right on time. Her stomach was tight as she pressed the button for the third floor. When the door slid open and she saw the plaque right outside, it clenched even more.

Sam Greentree, Attorney at Law.

She still had no idea why he'd called. Their phone conversation the day before had been brief, with him insisting that they talk in person.

For the past twenty-four hours, she'd done nothing but obsess about why some lawyer in Pasadena she'd never even heard of wanted to meet with her.

She had an idea, of course.

John Davis.

She opened the door to his office hesitantly, not sure what she'd find. But there was nothing on the other side but a small waiting room, occupied only by a bored-looking receptionist. The furnishings were tasteful but sparse: a brown leather couch, a round coffee table with neatly-stacked piles of *Architectural Digest*, a few seascapes decorating the beige walls.

Megan gave her name to the receptionist, who said that Mr. Greentree would be with her shortly. Then lowered herself onto the couch, noting how cool the leather felt against the backs of her thighs.

Her stomach was still in knots.

I *can't* be in trouble, she told herself, just as she had a thousand times since yesterday's phone call. If anyone planned to implicate me in his death, it's the cops who'd be contacting me, not some lawyer.

She grabbed a magazine and flipped through the pages, feigning interest in the stark rooms and the fanciful lighting fixtures. But in her head, she went over the story she'd constructed, the one she'd told the police. The story she'd repeated to herself so many times she almost accepted it as the truth.

That she and John Davis had first met while he was searching for a housesitter, instantly becoming friends. That after he returned from the short trip he'd been planning, the two of them were enjoying a swim in the pool. Horsing around a bit, with her climbing onto his shoulders and diving off them. That John had mentioned that he'd recently stopped taking one of his medications, going cold turkey—and he wondered if it had been a mistake, since he'd been feeling dizzy, even faint, at times.

She'd told the police she'd gone into the house to use the bathroom. Discovered him floating in the pool when she returned and immediately dialed 9-1-1.

The coroner's discovery that John's body contained traces of prednisone, coupled with the prednisone tablets found in the prescription bottle in the bathroom, fully supported her claim that John's death had been accidental. The coroner also concluded that the bruising on his shoulders was the result of her standing on them, using them for a diving board.

His finding was that John's death was the result of his own poor judgment.

Megan told herself that couldn't have been the reason she'd been summoned to this lawyer's office. And that a lawsuit was the next most obvious possibility. Maybe John had some relative who bore a grudge against her. She couldn't imagine why, but wasn't that the nature of lawsuits—that they could be over the most obscure, seemingly inconsequential thing?

As she distractedly turned another page of the magazine, she found herself hoping desperately that she was wrong, that the reason she was here today had nothing to do with John Davis and that whole hideous experience.

The last thing she wanted was to think about any of it. In fact, she'd spent the weeks since it had all happened trying to forget—or at least find a way to live with the horrible memories that continued to give her nightmares. Nightmares that were always the same: she was still trapped inside John's house.

That is, when she actually managed to fall asleep.

Since moving back to Elissa's, focusing on even the simplest thing had been impossible. Even looking for a job had been beyond her. Fortunately, Elissa had been as patient as ever. She'd never asked for details about what happened with her housesitting gig. Never asked Megan to chip in for the rent, either, as if she'd figured out that her savings were quickly draining away.

She jumped to her feet when a fiftyish man in an expensive-looking suit opened the door off the waiting area.

"Ms. Quinn?" he asked without a trace of a smile.

She nodded, then followed him into his office. It resembled the law offices on TV, with a big desk, two chairs opposite it, and dark wooden shelves lined with books that were all the same size.

She sat in one of the chairs and looked at him expectantly, wondering if he could hear her heart thumping in her chest.

"The reason I got in touch with you," he began without wasting time on pleasantries, "is John Davis's recent death."

Just hearing his name made her entire body tense up.

The lawyer folded his hands on his desk and leaned forward. "Just to satisfy my own curiosity, Ms. Quinn, how long did you know Mr. Davis?"

"Not that long," she answered woodenly.

"But the two of you were close?"

She was silent for a few seconds before saying, "We were . . . friends."

From the lawyer's clouded expression, Megan got the feeling he wasn't satisfied with her answers.

"Would you mind telling me what this is about?" she finally blurted out.

"What it's about," he replied slowly, "is Mr. Davis's will."

His response took her completely by surprise. Never in a million years would she have expected John to have named her in his will.

"Mr. Davis came in to see me last month, just a few days before his accident," the lawyer continued. "He insisted on changing it."

And then she understood.

"This is about his cat, isn't it?" she said. "I was hoping I'd be able to keep her. When he died in that tragic accident, taking her with me seemed like the obvious thing to do. "

"This isn't about his cat," the lawyer interrupted.

Megan stared at him, still puzzled.

"It's about his house." The corners of his mouth turned downward. "He left it to you."

She was still trying to comprehend the words she'd just heard when Sam Greentree added, "I don't know how much you know about real estate, especially in Pasadena, but that place is easily worth between two and three million dollars."

The meaning of the words had barely sunk in as he said, "There is one stipulation, however."

"A stipulation?" Megan repeated.

"And I should note that if you fail to comply, the house will be turned over to the Pasadena Animal Shelter."

"What's the stipulation?"

"It's related to the timing of putting the house on the market," the lawyer explained.

"I don't understand," she said.

He took a deep breath. "Mr. Davis stipulated that you are not to sell the house for a period of at least five years. During that time, you are to make it your primary residence.

"In other words," he said, "you have to live in John's house."

Dark Corridors is home to the best contemporary tales of mystery and suspense. For page turners that make your heart pound, your blood chill, explore our library of titles—but beware! Our shadowy hallways are full of unexpected twists and turns, eerie sights, unearthly sounds, and the ghosts of visitors who explored Dark Corridors before you ... *never to be seen again!*